# THE BRIDESMAID AND THE REALITY SHOW

Wedding Games: Book One

---

## KAYLA TIRRELL
## DAPHNE JAMES HUFF

# ONE

## 10 Days Until Dream Wedding

Sienna was late.

Her t-shirt was inside out.

And she had to pee.

This whole crazy trip was not off to a good start.

She still couldn't believe Audrey had agreed to be a participant in the show, *Wedding Games.* Or that it was filming near their hometown.

Sure, the idea of spending ten days in a gorgeous mountain inn with all expenses paid was tempting. And knowing it would all end in an over-the-top wedding—that was guaranteed to be the topic of Thanksgiving dinners for years to come—also sounded amazing.

But couldn't Audrey see that, for every reason to agree to be a participant in the show, there were a million other reasons to say no?

This was reality TV, after all. People weren't looking for a smooth, problem-free event. That was too boring—too easy. Viewers wanted drama. They wanted meltdowns.

And the producers of the show were going to make

sure their audience got what they wanted by any means necessary. At least, that was the argument Sienna had made when Audrey first called her with the news—an argument she'd voiced even louder once she'd seen the contract she was required to sign.

A film-crew would be allowed all access to the wedding preparations, and everyone in the wedding party needed to sign it if they wanted to be invited to the intimate ceremony. It was frustrating to be forced into a reality TV show, but Audrey was Sienna's sister, for goodness sake. She wouldn't dream of missing this wedding, so she signed the stupid thing, even though it was filled with so much legal jargon it made her head spin.

Everyone knew drama was what made people keep watching those shows. Viewers hoped the bride would go full-blown crazy. Or that one of the bridesmaids would get jealous of the way everyone fussed over the bride. It was a perfect storm, and Audrey couldn't see it.

But why would she listen to her little sister? It's not like Sienna had first-hand experience in the entertainment business—oh wait, yes, she did. Sure, it was only a few years, and mostly stage and commercial work, but she knew the industry better than the rest of her family. Maybe Audrey was too blinded by the idea of her happily ever after with Eli, so she didn't consider how difficult this might be for everyone else involved. Sienna had never been in love like that but had heard it made you do all sorts of crazy things.

Regardless, Sienna loved her sister and was going to support her. She'd packed her suitcase, booked a last-minute red-eye flight from New York to Asheville, and had just finished driving an hour to get to the secluded inn the producers chose for the filming site.

Growing up in the area, she'd never even known it was tucked away in the mountains. But someone from up north had bought it last year, and it was all her family could talk about. As the destination came into view, Sienna thought it looked more like a mansion that wanted to pretend it was something cozier.

It was a two-story building with large windows on every side that were sure to give the place the perfect amount of natural light any time of day. One side of the inn had an impressive stone chimney that took up the entire wall. And way in the distance, Sienna could see the corner of what looked to be an old barn, set against the backdrop of acres and acres of gorgeous trees and mountains.

With the sun still rising in the distance, the scene was magnificent.

Sienna drove up the gravel path and crossed her fingers that the rental car she'd gotten had enough power to make it up the steep incline to the front of the building. The bumpy road was not helping her bladder situation, which had reached critical levels about ten minutes ago.

She was the last to show up—as usual—and saw a small crowd that consisted of the wedding party gathered out front. The camera crew was still off to the side and mercifully hadn't begun filming yet, as far as she could tell. That meant she had time to take care of her pressing business.

She parked her car beside her mother's familiar and practical beige sedan.

With a deep sigh, and a mumbled, "you can do

this," Sienna looked in the rearview mirror. She plastered a fake smile on her face and stepped out of her vehicle.

Her mother came rushing over immediately, a look of panic across her face. "Oh, Sienna, there you are," she shrieked. "We've all been wondering if you would ever show up."

"And hello to you too, Mother," Sienna answered, the smile still affixed to her face. "Glad to see you made it here safe."

Her mother huffed as she planted both of her hands on her hips. "Where have you been? It's nearly nine."

A jolt of panic shot through her. "Isn't that what time the contract said to be here?" She could have gotten an earlier flight, but it would have made her miss two shifts at work and cost her two-hundred dollars more. Two-hundred dollars she most certainly did not have.

Her mother shook her head and let out another loud puff of air. "Well, just because they say nine, it doesn't mean that you have to cut it so close." She leaned in and lowered her voice. "You and I both know how much is at stake."

"I know."

The contract was so full of ways things could go badly, so it was hard for Sienna to know what exactly her mother was referring to. The right to defamation, the hold clause, the lack of privacy for them but confidentiality for the show. It was all to keep the power in the hands of the producers.

But failing to show up, well, that would potentially pull the plug on the whole thing. Sienna might be notorious for being late, but she wasn't going to risk putting her sister's wedding in jeopardy. Sienna had been so concerned with making it on time, she'd packed everything in a carry-on bag to avoid getting stuck at baggage claim and hadn't even stopped in the airport bathroom to pee before racing out the doors toward the rental car kiosks. The pressure on her bladder was downright unbearable at this point, and she had one mission: Find the little girls' room—STAT.

"Well, then let's go." Her mother put her hand on Sienna's shoulder and started to lead her to the rest of the group.

"Actually," Sienna pulled her phone from her back pocket, "I still have fifteen minutes, which means I have just enough time to go to the bathroom."

She pushed past her mother who was mumbling about her disorganized daughter and walked up to the front door of the inn. Nearby, everyone talked excitedly. In her rush, Sienna barely gave anyone more than a passing glance. She did, however, catch Audrey's raised eyebrows and subtle tap of her watch.

Sienna would have plenty of time to catch up, but for right now, she had one thing on her mind. It was like her body sensed a bathroom was close and had given up all hope of holding it in. If she didn't get to the toilet soon, she was going to give the camera crew a great opening shot.

It was exactly the kind of thing that would happen to her, and she doubted she'd be able to convince the producer not to air something that would provide so much comedy to the high-drama show. Not to mention it was just the kind of thing a casting director might hold against her in a future audition.

No one would hire her as a leading lady in a serious

role if ten million viewers had watched her wet her pants. The only thing to do after that would be—shudder—more reality TV. Sienna groaned at the thought as she picked up the pace with a renewed fervor.

After the receptionist at the front desk pointed to where the bathroom was, Sienna practically sprinted down the hall.

*Man, I really shouldn't have had so much coffee on the plane.*

When she rounded the corner, she bumped into a man, but she couldn't stop to apologize. She needed to pee right this second. He started to say something to her, but she couldn't stop to listen, not with her destination in sight. Sienna whipped the door open and locked herself in the bathroom, relieved to…well, relieve herself.

A moan escaped her mouth just as a light knock came at the door.

"Wait just a hot second!" she called.

A deep, male voice carried through the door. "I was just going to say—"

"Occupied!"

"—that it's out of toilet paper."

Sienna's eyes snapped to the toilet paper dispenser, and her heart sank as she saw that the man on the other side of the door was right. And, of course, the bathroom was one of those eco-friendly ones that used air-dryers instead of having a paper towel dispenser.

She sighed. Not only was she going to have to come up with some creative solutions, now there was someone else who was going to be privy to it. In her rush, she hadn't noticed much about the person, but he sounded like a cranky old man.

She sent up a silent prayer. *Please don't let them be part of the* Wedding Games *crew.*

That would be a sure-fire way to put a target on her head for the entire week.

After figuring out the not-so-convenient logistics of cleaning up without toilet paper, Sienna washed her hands and wiped them on her jeans, too impatient to wait for the weak trickle of hot air to dry them. She ran her fingers through her blonde hair and gave herself a quick once-over before she left the small bathroom. Tilting her head to the side, she pulled her compact out of her purse. It wasn't clear if there would be makeup artists. Reality show or not, there was no way she could be filmed with those bags under her eyes.

Another knock interrupted her concealer application. "Are you okay? Didn't fall in or anything, did you?"

What was this guy's problem?

She put her makeup back in her purse, and opened the bathroom door, ready to give him a piece of her mind. But when she stepped into the hall, she pulled up short. The cranky old man was, in fact, a gorgeous young man. His dark hair barely brushed the tops of the light blue eyes that were looking directly at her. He was dressed in a simple plaid shirt and jeans that gave away his position as property maintenance—possibly a handyman.

He grinned as he pushed himself off the wall and held out two rolls of toilet paper. "I thought you might need these."

It was too bad those ridiculously good looks didn't come with any sense. It was common courtesy not to interrupt someone while they were going to the bathroom—or wait outside until they were done.

Sienna looked down at the two rolls with a sneer. "And what? You thought you were just going to bring them in while I was going to the bathroom?"

The guy's smile evaporated. "Sorry for trying to be helpful. I'd hoped to get them to you in time."

Sienna rolled her eyes. "Well, you did a terrible job."

"I did the best I could considering you ran past me and ignored me as I tried to explain."

"And then you thought it would be a good idea to hang out on the other side of the door? You do know that's, like, creep level ten, right?"

Hurt flashed across his face for the briefest moment before he shook his head. "You know what? I'm not going to stand here and be berated for wanting to help."

With one last pointed look in her direction, the guy stormed off. Sienna stayed glued in her spot and gave him a head start. With any luck, she wouldn't see him again. She'd simply avoid the places where custodians usually hung out and hope he didn't blab about the rude girl to the rest of the staff. She crossed her fingers she wouldn't find any surprises in her clean sheets tonight.

After waiting in the hall for what she felt was an appropriate amount of time, Sienna joined everyone outside. She ignored the questioning look her mother gave her as she walked over to where Audrey and their middle sister, Harper, were chatting.

Humor danced in Audrey's deep, brown eyes. "You drank too much coffee, didn't you?"

Sienna smiled back at her sister. She knew her addictions well. "Obviously."

"Well, I'm just glad you're here," Audrey said with a quick hug. "I know you weren't too happy about the contract."

"Of course I'm here." At least *all* her comments over the past few weeks hadn't been totally ignored. "I wouldn't miss your wedding for anything."

"Mother was about to have a coronary," Harper added. "I swear she checked the time every minute until you got here. I was afraid she was going to call the police to start a search party for you."

Sienna snorted. "It's a wedding. It's not like it's a hair appointment. Even I know how important…"

Her words died off as she spotted a familiar face in the crowd. True, there were a lot of familiar faces here. The group consisted of family and close friends, along with the production crew. There were her sisters and Audrey's best friend, and maid of honor, Reagan. Reagan's fiancé Harry was talking on his phone off to the side.

But this face was familiar because Sienna had seen it outside the bathroom only moments earlier.

"Audrey, what's the custodian doing next to Eli?" she asked.

Audrey craned her neck to look around at Eli's parents. "What are you talking about?"

Sienna let out an impatient huff. "The guy with the dark hair who is literally standing next to Eli. Plaid shirt, blue eyes. Why is he out here?"

"Uh, Sienna." Audrey furrowed her brow. "The only person I see over there is Fox. He's Eli's best friend from college."

Eli's best friend? No, that couldn't be right. Even though Sienna lived in New York, she'd met Eli plenty of times. Plus, she followed him on social media like a good future sister-in-law, and not once had she ever seen this Fox guy. She'd remember someone like that. Those eyes weren't exactly something you forget.

Her heart quickened beneath her ribs. "Are you sure?" Sienna asked, her eyes still trained on the guy she'd just argued with as he stood next to Eli.

The two men both wore easy smiles as they talked.

"Are you seriously asking me if I know who my husband-to-be's best man is?"

Best man? Sienna's stomach plummeted. This was so not good.

"Why are you so concerned about the"—Harper lifted her hands and made air quotes—"custodian anyway?"

Sienna felt her cheeks warm. "He was standing outside the bathroom with toilet paper, and I thought he worked here." She cleared her throat. "I may have been rude to him."

Audrey frowned at her. "Oh, Sienna, you didn't."

She explained what had happened inside, only realizing how quick she'd been to make judgements and serve out punishments once she said it all out loud. A pang of remorse ran through her. She'd acted like a jerk.

Audrey's face was stern, but Harper laughed and waggled her brows. "Looks like the producers won't have to work too hard to get must-see TV from you."

"Shut up." Sienna pushed her sister. "I'm sure I can make it through ten days. This is Audrey's special moment."

She needed to remain in control of her emotions whenever a camera was in view. This was her chance to get noticed, but given the expectations of reality shows, it had to be for all the right reasons. There'd be chances to sing and dance, and opportunities to show off her emotional range. One hint of drama and she could kiss any chance at a real career goodbye.

And time was running out on a real career. Sienna and her roommate were skating on thin ice—one more late rent payment and goodbye New York. This reality show was the last thing Sienna wanted to do but was her only chance to hold on to her dreams.

She could make it through ten days without any drama, right?

## TWO

## 10 Days Until Dream Wedding

Fox watched the rude girl from the bathroom walk over to where Audrey and Harper stood. Once the third girl took her place beside them, they looked like Russian nesting dolls—all fair-skinned, blonde hair, and slightly staggered heights. It would be comical if Fox wasn't so irritated about his earlier interaction with the newcomer.

The pit forming in Fox's stomach already knew the answer, but he had to ask. "Who's that girl standing next to Audrey?"

Eli turned to where his future bride stood laughing at something one of the other girls had said. "Which one?"

*The prettiest one,* Fox almost said, but caught himself. "The one in the blue tank top."

Eli chuckled. "Oh, yeah. That's Sienna. She's Audrey's youngest sister. Basically, everything you'd expect from the baby of the family."

The baby. That sounded about right from what he'd seen so far. Plus, she looked at least ten years younger than Fox, which would put her in her early twenties. Girls that age had more beauty than sense, in his experience.

But, just to be sure…

"What do you mean 'everything you'd expect from the baby'?" he asked, peeling his eyes away from where she stood and back to Eli.

"Only that she's a bit of a drama queen. Loves attention. Moved to New York right after college to pursue an acting career."

Ha! He'd been right about her age. The acting thing fit too. She was a picture-perfect, spoiled cele-brat. "Actress, huh? Been in anything good?" He lifted his brows.

"If you call an off-off Broadway play that even Audrey wanted to bail on early and a three-episode run on a second-rate crime drama 'good,' then sure." Eli shrugged. "It's cool though, she's got a big heart and enough grit. She's been working, like, three part-time jobs or something the past year but she doesn't let it get her down. She's convinced she's a star."

Fox laughed to himself. "Yeah, I can see that."

A line formed between Eli's brows. "What do you mean?"

"Nothing."

Eli gave him a questioning look, but thankfully Fox was saved from having to explain any further by an unnatural hush that spread through the small crowd gathered outside.

A middle-aged man walked up the oversized steps that led to the front of the inn. His slicked back, dark brown hair was sprinkled with gray. He wore a suit that said, "Look at me, I'm important." But the power that radiated off the man was enough to command attention even if he had been wearing old jeans and a ratty t-shirt.

"Good morning, everyone!" He flashed them all a blindingly white Hollywood smile. "My name is Bruce, the executive producer for *Wedding Games*. Now that we're all here, I'd like to go over some last-minute things you should know."

What else was there to know about being on a reality show besides "bring all the drama" and "leave your brains and dignity at the door"? This was as close to a nightmare as Fox could imagine. But after everything Eli had done for him over the years, Fox had said yes without hesitation. That didn't mean he hadn't read the contract about fourteen times. After all the mistakes he'd made in the past, he'd wanted to make sure he knew exactly what he was getting into before he signed on the dotted line.

"The filming for *Wedding Games* starts at dinner tonight. We'll have everyone gather into the meeting room, and then the host of the show, Jason Castle, will go over some of the challenges."

There was a sudden rush of excited whispers at the name of the host. Fox vaguely remembered seeing him on TV as a kid, thinking he was pretty cool. Now he just looked old.

"What kind of challenges?" said a female voice from the crowd. Fox didn't have to turn his head to know who it was. Not only was the voice familiar, but based on what he'd observed, and what Eli had just told him about Audrey's youngest sister, there was only one person it could be.

"And ruin the surprise?" Bruce's mouth curved into

a smile. "Sorry, but we're hoping to catch authentic reactions from everyone."

"Authentic reactions?"

Bruce's smile tightened to a thin line. "We know none of you are professional actors or actresses." Fox turned his head just in time to see the scowl on Sienna's face. "We're not looking for you to feign shock, joy, or even anger. We want you to be yourselves."

Fox shook his head at the young woman's reaction. Someone must have forgotten to tell the producer that he was in the presence of Broadway's next rising star.

Bruce's jaw clenched slightly before his smile returned. "You'll also be happy to know we set up one room on the bottom floor as a safe space. There's a sign labeling it as such. This is the one room no cameras will be allowed. We encourage you to use this room sparingly."

He paused and lifted an eyebrow, making sure they understood "sparingly" meant "never." When he opened his mouth to start speaking again, the same female voice from earlier called out again.

"They'll get a nice wedding no matter what, right?"

A chorus of groans went through the crowd, and Fox turned his head once more to where the three sisters stood. The other two were both whispering something in Sienna's ears.

She shook her head and stood her ground.

"Don't worry, Miss...?" The producer waited for Sienna to answer.

"Sienna Hudson."

"Ah, yes. Of course. The youngest sister to Audrey, and one of the three bridesmaids, correct?"

Sienna nodded, but mercifully kept her mouth shut.

Fox looked back up toward the producer.

"The contract clearly states that so long as everyone respects the duties outlined in the contract, Eli and Audrey will get their wedding, all expenses paid, at the end of the ten days." He cleared his throat, the thin, tight smile back on his lips. "And if there are no further questions, you're dismissed. Take this time to get settled into your rooms, take a walk around the property, whatever you wish. Just make sure you report to the office next to the meeting room at noon for hair and makeup."

Bruce gave one last pointed look in Sienna's direction before marching back down the stairs and over to where the camera crew stood. Bruce launched into giving directions to them, pointing several times to the sisters.

Eli wasn't kidding when he called Sienna the drama queen of the family. Not only was she rude, but she spoke too quickly, without thinking about what it might mean for others. Though he'd known her for less than thirty minutes, he wasn't too eager to see what other flaws she had up her sleeve—not that he should care. Normally he wouldn't, but if her big, fat mouth ruined his best friend's special day, he wasn't going to be very happy about it.

He mentally poured over the contract he had signed when he agreed to come on this show for Eli. There were so many clauses, and each one could be broken. He imagined all the ways Sienna could mess things up. Would she try to make this all about her?

He startled when a firm hand gripped his shoulder. "Don't worry about the makeup."

Fox looked up at his best friend. "Huh?"

"You look concerned, but don't worry about it. Even

male reporters wear makeup when they're in front of the camera. I'm sure they won't make you look like a clown." Eli chuckled.

Fox nodded, still distracted by the contract. "Yeah, I'm sure it's gonna be fine. I'm just feeling a little on edge. Bruce made me uncomfortable. Did you notice the way he stormed off?"

"I'm sure he's just not used to being interrupted by people."

Fox raised his brows. "And that's why I am concerned. Hopefully, Audrey's little sister doesn't ruin the wedding."

"Ruin the wedding?" Eli snorted. "You're going to have to relax, man."

"How can anyone relax? It's reality TV. It's like you and Audrey have gone completely crazy."

"Look, I know everyone is a little freaked out about us agreeing to do the show. But weddings are expensive, and we're scraping by on two teacher's salaries. We basically have to decide if we want to get married or buy a house."

"Have you considered waiting on the house?"

"Of course we have, but now we don't have to." Eli grinned. "Not only is the network paying for everything this week, they've also agreed to pay for the honeymoon."

"And doesn't that make you a little wary? They aren't putting up that much cash for purely altruistic reasons, you know."

"I know," Eli said with a sigh. "But I love Audrey, and I want to give her the wedding she deserves."

Fox resisted rolling his eyes, but just barely. Eli had been this gooey eyed for Audrey since college. He should be used to it by now. "And you're prepared for the reality show drama that's sure to follow?"

Eli smiled. "No matter what challenges get thrown our way, when it's all done, I'm going to be the happiest man on Earth because I'll be married to the love of my life."

The level of cheesiness of his best friend was getting out of control, and the cameras hadn't even started filming.

"And if this week is really hard, that's okay too, because we'll be sipping strawberry daiquiris in Mexico while everyone else goes back to their day jobs."

"Well, you could at least pretend to feel bad for everyone else." Fox shook his head. "Show some remorse?"

"Not a chance," Eli answered. "Now let's go grab our bags. We don't have long before they start painting our faces."

———

TWO HOURS LATER, bags unpacked and makeup applied, Fox and the rest of the wedding party stood outside the inn's meeting room. There were several people on the production crew standing with them, easily identifiable by the lanyards around their necks that read, *Wedding Games* in repeating print. Bruce was nowhere to be seen, and Fox thought that was for the best as Sienna walked up.

He tried to ignore her as she loudly complained to her sisters about having to go to hair and makeup.

"I've been doing my makeup for as long as I can remember." She huffed. "I know which products make my face look shiny and which ones match my skin tone, thank you very much."

"You look fine, Sienna," Audrey said in a hushed tone, but Sienna continued to complain.

"No, I look all washed out. I'm going to look like a vampire on screen."

Her protests were met with laughter from her sisters. He had no clue why they allowed her to act this way when they were about to walk into something as major as planning Eli and Audrey's wedding on television. What Fox did know was that he couldn't stand it anymore.

He turned to tell Sienna to stop being so selfish, expecting to see the same girl who had bumped into him on her way to the bathroom, but when his eyes met hers, he was struck silent.

While she was technically the same girl from earlier —blonde hair, fair skin, bright eyes—the makeup artists had somehow transformed her appearance. Her blonde hair fell in gentle waves around her glowing face, her blue eyes somehow impossibly brighter than earlier. As much as he hadn't wanted to admit it due to his irritation, she'd been stunning before; this was literally movie star beautiful.

Her gaze met his, and he swore a slight blush hit her cheeks, though it could have been another enhancement from whatever they'd put on her skin. Fox's breath caught in his chest, and through muddled thoughts of how gorgeous she was, he managed to remind himself just who this girl was.

She was Sienna Hudson, sister of the bride-to-be.

By the end of their time here, she would be Fox's best friend's sister-in-law. She was completely off limits, and beyond that, she was everything he wanted to distance himself from. She was overly dramatic, only cared about herself, and the smile that touched her lips at his interested gaze was just a little too bright and wide to be real.

And yet, he couldn't tear his eyes away from her. It was as if the longer he stood taking her in, the more impossible it became to stop looking at her.

"Is there a problem?" She had a hand on her hip, and her perfectly groomed eyebrows were high on her forehead.

Okay, not entirely impossible. Her rudeness was enough to pull him out of the embarrassing trance she'd put on him.

"Just amazed they managed to make you look like a human, not a plastic doll."

Her eyes narrowed, and she opened her mouth to reply, but was interrupted by a crewmember clearing her throat. Fox quickly glanced around the small crowd to see if anyone else had noticed their brief interaction but felt confident everyone was too caught up in the excitement to care.

"Okay, folks. Here's how it's going to work," said a young woman with a long, dark ponytail and a badge that read "Jennifer: Production Assistant." She waited until everyone was quiet before continuing. "We're going to have everyone walk into the meeting room. Without giving too much away, I'll just say this: If you're a bridesmaid, you're part of the bride's family. If you're a groomsman, you're considered part of the groom's family. Do you understand?"

Fox nodded along with everyone else.

"Good." The woman smiled. "The next thing is, try

not to look directly at the cameras. As we proceed through the next ten days, you'll get better at ignoring them, but we need to make sure we have enough footage of the first day. To help you, I'll just tell you now that there is one in the very front of the room and two set on either side of the room. Got it?"

Another wave of nods from everyone.

"Good. Then, ready or not, let the games begin."

At these words, some of the other production staff opened the double doors leading to the meeting room.

The first thing Fox noticed was the brightness of it all. There were lights and those weird umbrella things everywhere that made his eyes hurt. The second thing Fox noticed was the way they'd transformed the meeting room into what now looked like a church sanctuary. There were faux pews on either side, and a trail of flower petals strewn in the path leading to the front of the room where there was a camera pointed directly at them.

Fox tried to train his eyes anywhere but at it, but the more he focused on not looking, the harder it became. Every muscle in his body felt tense as he walked up to where the show's host stood smiling brightly just in front of the camera.

"Welcome to *Wedding Games*," Jason Castle said as everyone slowly made their way to where he stood in a black tuxedo. "As is customary, we'll have the bride on the left and the groom on the right."

Everyone awkwardly found their places as their host continued. He droned on about love being the thing that holds us together and how when you find that special someone you want to make it last.

Just another flashy reminder of how fake this entire production was.

"We have five games, competitions if you will, that will each determine a different aspect of the wedding." At this, Fox stood straighter. "The bridesmaids versus the groomsmen. Whoever wins each competition will get to pick the flowers, music, menu, bridesmaid dresses, and cake."

*Ah.* And now the catch to the "dream wedding" was out in the open. Not knowing what the competitions were—or the options, for that matter—Fox was already imagining the Frankensteined wedding that would be waiting for his best friend when everything was said and done.

He looked around and wondered if anyone truly knew what they were getting themselves into. But if the excitement on everyone's faces was any indication, he was the only one who had first-hand experience with how glamourous fame could appear, and just how horrible it could be behind the scenes.

## THREE

## 10 Days Until Dream Wedding

---

*NONE of you are professional actors or actresses.*

Sienna hadn't been able to get those stupid words out of her head ever since Bruce had spoken them during their first meeting. He seemed to know a lot about Sienna, which was normal since they'd done background checks on all of them. But if that were the case, he'd know that Sienna *was*, in fact, a professional actor —and how she hated the term actress.

Just because she'd only had a few roles didn't make her any less legitimate. She'd spent a fortune when she first moved to New York on acting classes in the city. She'd practiced with the best vocal coaches, studied so many videos of the greats she often dreamed of their facial expressions, and went to every open call and casting audition in the tri-state area.

If that wasn't professional, she didn't know what was.

Although, technically, Bruce was the professional here, even if his current stint making reality TV made Sienna want to gag. And his name did seem vaguely familiar, though she couldn't quite place it. Too bad a production assistant had taken their phones at the door so they wouldn't buzz accidentally during the all-important introduction scene, because Sienna wanted to look him up. She made a mental note to do it later. Who knew? Maybe she recognized the name because he'd been working on one of the hundreds of commercials she'd auditioned for.

Bruce's words had echoed through her mind as the show's host went over the basic concept of the show, and they echoed through her head now as the girls on the "bride's team" waited in an empty room to conduct their initial video diaries.

The team consisted of Audrey, Harper, Sienna, and the maid-of-honor. Even though Reagan was the only non-relative in the small group, it didn't feel that way to Sienna. In fact, Reagan had been Audrey's best friend for so long now, that it almost felt like she was the fourth sister they never had—even with her fiery red hair and tall frame.

Just as Sienna started to wonder if they were keeping them waiting just to see how long it would take for them to start complaining, Bruce walked in with a cameraman by his side. She straightened in her seat. This man was the producer, not some peon.

*So why is he the one conducting the interviews?*

Sienna pushed the sinking feeling of unease aside as she plastered on the brightest smile she could muster. When she turned to the other three girls, frustration bubbled up at their lack of enthusiasm. Audrey and Reagan both wore matching demure grins on their faces, while Harper was staring intently at the production crew in the corner and barely registered the room's new additions.

*Oh well*, she thought to herself. *I guess I'll just have to be captivating enough for everyone.*

Sienna shifted in her seat as Bruce sat down across from them and put the clipboard he was carrying in his lap. She mentally went over every part of her posture. Chin up, back straight, shoulders relaxed, legs crossed at the ankle, hands resting casually in her lap. She had practiced this pose in front of her mirror so many times, it felt almost natural to her now.

Not that it mattered how it felt. All Sienna cared about was how it made her look for the camera—the one being manned by a baby face who she could only hope knew how to capture her best angle. This was her chance to be seen, and she couldn't afford to have anyone mess it up for her.

"Good afternoon, ladies," Bruce said.

"Good afternoon," Sienna said brightly.

Audrey just smiled in response, and Harper's muffled "hi" came a half second too late.

Sienna bit the side of her tongue but kept her smile plastered on.

"From time to time, I like to sit down with the different contestants to see how everyone is feeling. They make great cut-away footage and voice-over clips, but please don't feel anxious about it. I want this to be comfortable—easy—just like a conversation with an old friend."

Sienna struggled to keep her smile natural while he said this. Bruce was not their friend; he was in the business of making good TV. But that didn't mean this couldn't be a mutually beneficial exchange.

"Let's start with something easy, shall we?" Bruce paused and smiled. "What do you guys think about the property?"

Sienna's shoulders relaxed a fraction of an inch. That *was* an easy one.

"It's beautiful," Sienna answered enthusiastically, realizing too late that Bruce was looking at Audrey. Lackluster or not, this whole thing was about the bride-to-be.

Sienna felt a slight warmth to her cheeks as she turned to face her sister. The kind, but gently reproving look Audrey gave her only made it worse.

"My sister is right," Audrey answered. "It *is* beautiful. The Emerald Inn will be the perfect place to marry Eli."

"And speaking of Eli, why don't you tell us a little about how the two of you met," Bruce said.

Audrey started into the story that Sienna had heard a million times. She knew it by heart now.

It was love at first sight.

They'd met in college but not at some random party. On the very first day of classes, they'd both been in the registrar's office, begging to switch out of an 8 a.m. math class. When they realized the hottie at the next counter would be in that class, they both decided to keep it. They'd been inseparable ever since.

While Audrey talked about how she and Eli had decided to pursue teaching degrees together, Sienna wondered what it would be like to know you wanted to spend the rest of your life with someone after meeting them only once.

An endless string of less-than-stellar dates with guys in the city had pretty much quashed any lingering hopes of the kind of romance her big sister's story had inspired in her teenage self.

It was like no one got her. When she tried dating fellow actors it always felt like a competition—who went on more auditions, who got the callback, who was the prettiest. It was tough when the guy you were dating spent more time in the bathroom getting ready than you did and then expected you to shower him with compliments.

But when Sienna tried to spend time with the more serious finance and lawyer guys from the city, they always talked down to her. They never took her acting seriously. One time, her date actually patted her on the head like she was a small child. It was humiliating and only made her more determined to get her big break.

"And it must be nice to have your sisters here for your big day," Bruce said, pulling Sienna from her thoughts.

"There are no other people I'd rather share this day with than these girls," Audrey said. She first turned to Sienna with a serene smile on her face.

Sienna gave her a playful wink.

Then Audrey turned to Harper—presumably with the same smile—but Harper was staring at her hands. Sienna watched as Audrey reached out and grabbed it, giving it a squeeze.

Harper's eyes snapped up, and she gave Audrey a quick grin. "We wouldn't miss it for the world."

"And Reagan?" Bruce asked.

Audrey lifted a shoulder. "She's my best friend, the sister I never knew I needed. I'm thankful she's here and honored to have her as my maid of honor."

"Ah, you do care," Reagan teased, and Audrey stuck her tongue out at her.

The playful interaction came at the perfect moment. Audrey's eyes were starting to look glassy, and things were feeling overly heartwarming—even for a reality show about weddings.

"And what about Milo?"

All the air whooshed out of Sienna's lungs. The smile she'd had been holding for ten minutes dropped.

*Come on, Sienna. You're better than this.*

She tried to lift the corner of her mouth, but it was no use. She'd just given Bruce the authentic reaction he'd wanted, and there was no recovery.

Sienna quickly glanced at the other three girls and found that they were in similar states of shock. Not only shock, but sadness. The kind of grief that comes from not talking to your brother for ten years.

Sienna's surprise was quickly replaced with anger when she turned toward Bruce. Unlike them, his expression was one of pure glee. Bruce had done his research on the entire Hudson clan. He'd pulled up as much dirt as he could on every single member of the family.

*Did he know something about where Milo was?*

Sienna couldn't think about him right now. She needed to fix this. Audrey was the bride-to-be, and she shouldn't have to worry about Milo. Harper was looking down at her stupid hands again. And Reagan, well, she was prettier than most actresses Sienna knew, but right now she looked more like a fish with her mouth flapping helplessly open and closed.

No, it was up to Sienna to do something.

She took a steadying breath, trying not to focus on

the angle she was being filmed, and gave Bruce her fiercest look.

His grin only grew.

Sienna fought to keep her expression consistent and gently clenched her hands at her sides. They would not be discussing Milo with Bruce. Milo's sudden departure was too painful, and not any of Bruce's business. It had nothing to do with this wedding or the next several days. "Next question."

"Sure thing." Bruce paused and cocked his head. "Audrey just told us all about Eli and how they met, but I'm curious to hear what everyone thinks about the rest of the groomsmen."

The other girls relaxed but Sienna stayed tense.

"For example, Fox Lynch." Bruce looked down at the clipboard for the first time during their interviews, though Sienna suspected he didn't need it. "He's Eli's best friend and best man."

Audrey beamed. "That's right."

"Why don't you tell us a little bit about him?"

It took all of Sienna's training to keep the surprise off her face as Audrey started to detail all the ways Fox was amazing. Loyal and trustworthy?

More like grumpy and withdrawn. When he wasn't mocking and rude, that is.

The entire time they'd been filming in the meeting room he'd been frowning, standing with his arms crossed over his stupid, wide, muscular chest. The best man looking like he wanted nothing to do with the wedding was exactly the kind of drama that would have people buzzing around the water cooler.

At least Audrey's glowing review of Fox wouldn't play into that storyline too much.

"He's been through so much, Eli's been like a brother to him. Eli, Fox, Wade, and M——" She paused and cleared her throat. "The three of them were all super close in college."

Bruce's lips lifted slightly at the almost mention of Milo. Sienna sighed, knowing he'd end up splicing this together into something horrible.

"Harry has fit right in with them." Reagan jumped in, trying to cover for Audrey. "Who knows, maybe I'll have all the same four guys at my wedding in a few months."

They all laughed, and Bruce made a signal that made the cameraman drop his camera.

"Thank you, ladies, that was great. Time for me to go find those guys and see if they have such nice things to say about you." He winked, and Sienna suppressed a shudder.

"That wasn't so bad," said Audrey once Bruce and the cameraman were gone. "I think this will go great, don't you?"

Sienna only wished the smile she gave her sister could be a real one.

## FOUR

## 10 Days Until Dream Wedding

Fox closed his eyes and took a deep breath, concentrating on the pool stick in his hand and the shot he was about to take. He opened his eyes, pulled his arm back and—

"Those sisters are quite something, aren't they?"

His concentration totally shattered by Bruce's question, Fox's shot went wide, and he cursed under his breath. What was the point of filming them while shooting pool if he was going to interrupt them with questions every two seconds?

"They're great," said Eli. "It's such an honor to become part of such an amazing family of strong women."

He was the picture of a relaxed, handsome groom-to-be, with his short cropped blond hair and bright smile, leaning casually against his stick that he'd propped against the floor.

Fox ran a hand through his slightly-too-long shaggy hair. He usually kept it short, but work had been crazy in the weeks leading up to this trip. The last time it had been this long was college, and unlike most people, he did not want to relive his college days.

"The Hudson women have had to be strong through many losses, right?" Bruce's eyes gleamed.

Eli's face fell, and Fox scowled. Fox had read the contract enough times to know there hadn't been a clause about divulging all your darkest secrets on television. They could cut and paste however they wanted but if you didn't reveal too much, they couldn't do too much damage. Fox's survival plan was to say as little as possible. And if Eli was smart, he'd keep his mouth shut too.

"Fox, your turn." Wade smacked his arm with his pool stick, and Fox poked him back. Wade's eyes lit with mischief, and Fox scooted away from him around the pool table. The friendly scuffle that ensued was distraction enough from the question, and Bruce turned to Harry.

Fox caught Eli's grateful look and shrugged. As much as Fox didn't want to be on camera, he wasn't about to let Eli get eaten alive by this bloodsucker producer.

"Reagan seems like a nice addition to their little trio." Bruce's smile was all teeth and no heart. "A little red firecracker I bet, huh?"

"Oh, I know how to keep her in her place." Harry exchanged a smug wink with Bruce.

Fox had to ball his hands into fists to stop from doing something stupid.

Who talked about such a sweet girl like that? Fox had known Reagan since college. Not as well as Audrey, but she'd been there throughout everything that had happened, and Fox was loyal to those who were loyal to him.

And it was only because of that loyalty that he did not give Harry the black eye he deserved right now. Messing around with Wade was one thing, but Eli and Audrey did not need a fight to break out. Even though Bruce would be sure to love it, Fox wasn't here to make the sleazy producer happy. He was here to make sure his friends got the best wedding ever.

Bruce turned back to Eli and the questions calmed down a bit, focusing on how he'd met Audrey and their early days of dating. It was pretty classic, cheesy, love story stuff. Fox turned his attention back to the game, ignoring the cameraman hovering just a little too close.

Fox gave one-word answers to his dumb questions like "Any guesses what's in store for the first challenge tomorrow?" and "How's it feel to see your best friend get married?" He'd hoped it would give Bruce the hint he wasn't going to play his games, but the gleam in the producer's eye left Fox feeling unsettled.

Finally, after what seemed like hours, Bruce and the cameramen left.

Fox took a deep breath as the door closed behind them. Nine more days to go after today.

"Finally," Eli said, coming to stand between Fox and Wade and slapping them both on the shoulder. "Now let's play some real pool."

Harry was looking down at his phone. "Sorry guys, I have work to do."

"This is supposed to be like a vacation for you guys," said Eli. "Enjoy the mountains a little in between filming."

"This can't wait, sorry." Harry strolled out of the room without even looking up from his phone.

"Who does that guy think he is?" asked Fox.

Reagan's fiancé had been a last-minute addition when Eli's coworker had pulled out for a family emergency. So far, Fox had been less than impressed with the guy. "We're all missing work this week."

"Not me." Eli grinned. "Should have been a teacher like me. Summer vacation for the win."

"Low pay, no respect, and snotty teenagers all day?" Wade laughed. "No thanks."

"And weren't you just complaining last week that half your summer is taken up by classes so you can stay certified?" added Fox, crossing his arms and shaking his head.

Eli waved away their comments with his hand. "Yeah, yeah...but I love what I do. Can either of you say the same?"

Fox felt the familiar pang of longing that hadn't gone away, even after ten years. He had loved his job a long time ago. Not anymore.

"Well, I for one am happy to be enjoying the mountains this week," said Wade. "A nice break from sitting behind my desk. Care to give us a tour?"

Eli led them out of the game room and out the front door to the cool summer evening.

Fox inhaled the earthy mountain air and felt his body relax a little. This was a big reason he'd said yes to this crazy plan. Hanging out with his best friends in a place he loved. Every time he came to visit Eli in this tiny town on the other side of the state, he felt the rest of the world, and his worries, melt away.

The three friends joked and laughed as they made their way across the wide lawn to the barn at the very back of the property. Wellspring was so different from the beach town where he lived these days. The biggest difference being that he didn't hate it here.

Instead of salt on the air and relentless blue skies, everything here was green. The grass was green, and the mountains that shot up on every horizon were covered in green trees. He was lucky to catch a sliver of blue through their branches on some parts of the property. It made him feel cozy and secure, like a warm, green blanket.

The only thing he liked better was getting lost in the hustle and bustle of a big city, but he had no good reason to go there, so he found as many excuses as he could to make the seven-hour drive from the coast to the mountains.

"So, these competitions," Eli said, and Fox's attention snapped back to the reason they were here—the wedding. "Honestly, I don't care about much except the cake and the music. Let the girls win the rest, but Audrey has terrible taste in music."

Fox chuckled. This was an undeniable truth. The girl was smart and funny and beautiful but had seriously zero appreciation for good music. He had done his best over the years to help her, but she was a lost cause.

"Also, I want a simple chocolate cake, and I know Harper will convince her to do something crazy like almond truffle lavender poppy seed."

They laughed. The stories of Harper's flavor combinations were notorious. And even though Fox had only been down to visit the Flour Girl Bakery a couple of times since coming to Wellspring, he noticed she had some unusual items in addition to the more normal offerings of pastries and bread.

"Either of you want to claim dibs on the garter

toss?" Eli said. "That's the only competition I really want to see who wins."

"Are you having one?" Wade asked.

Eli shrugged. "Who knows, but it could be fun to see you both try to catch it."

"Seriously?" Fox asked. A pine-scented breeze ruffled his hair and he ran a hand through it. "Harper and Sienna are the only available girls."

And they were both definitely off limits.

"And what's wrong with them?" Wade kicked at a branch that had fallen across their path. "I kind of assumed you'd be looking to hook up with one of them."

"No way," Fox said and stopped in his tracks.

They'd made it all the way around the back of the barn and had started down a path through the trees. Eli had promised a great viewpoint up ahead, but night was coming soon, and Fox worried about being able to navigate back to the inn in the dark.

Of course, given the choice between spending the night in the woods or more time in front of the cameras—and around Sienna—Fox knew which one he'd pick.

"Why not? Sienna is adorable," said Wade.

"Then why don't you go for her?" Fox countered.

"Nah, you know she's not my type," Wade said. "Plus, she's in the entertainment business, so I thought you guys may have a lot in common."

"I thought I had a lot in common with Becky too."

Eli and Wade looked appropriately disgusted at the mention of Fox's college girlfriend. The one who'd betrayed him and broken his heart in every possible way.

The one who looked and acted *exactly* like Sienna.

"She is nothing like Becky," said Eli. "Sure, she's a

little overly dramatic when she's with her family and knows she can get away with it. But she's been in the city for a few years now and still has her head on straight. She's a good kid."

Fox laughed. "'Kid' being the operative word here. She's going to wake up one day and realize the world doesn't revolve around her, and it'll be the end of her."

"Wow, harsh, dude," said Wade. "You just met her this morning and said what, all of ten words to her? Give her a chance."

Fox shook his head. Spending more time with that beautiful, shallow woman would just remind him of when he had been that young and hopeful and stupid.

"She's not the maid of honor, so I won't really see much of her, will I?" Fox was snapping off leaves from branches along the path. "They'll probably pair me up with Reagan for stuff."

"Maybe," said Eli, suddenly running ahead on the trail. "Look, we're here."

Stepping around the final bank of trees, the three friends stood on an outcropping of rocks, looking over a green valley on fire in the golden evening light.

"Wow." Fox and Wade laughed at their identical breathless reactions to the view.

"Are you sure you guys don't want me to find you a teaching gig at my school?" Eli grinned. He spread his arms out wide. "You could be looking at this every day instead of the asphalt jungle or smelling fish on the docks."

All the happiness left Fox at the reminder of his miserable job, but before he could dwell on those feelings, a woman he recognized as Audrey's mom came rushing around the turn in the path.

Emily Hudson had the same fair skin and blonde hair as her daughters, only the smile lines around her lips were more defined ,and her crow's feet were more noticeable. Other than that, she could have been the smallest of the little Russian nesting dolls he had imagined earlier.

"There you are," she cried and entered the clearing with a cameraman close behind. She quickly walked over to where Eli stood, grabbed his face, and kissed his cheek. "Everyone is looking for you."

Eli looked down at his watch with a good-natured smile. "What do you mean everyone is looking for us? I didn't think we were supposed to be down there until six."

A blush hit Emily's cheeks. "Fine, not everyone. But I was outside walking around the property while Bruce interviewed the girls, and I met the owners of this place. They're a young couple just like you, and I thought you might like to meet them."

A quick glance in Eli's direction told Fox that he most certainly did not want to meet some random couple that happened to own the Emerald Inn, but Eli nodded and said "sure" anyway.

"Then, come on," Emily said, and grabbed Eli's hand to drag him away.

Fox lagged behind on the trail as Mrs. Hudson and Eli shuffled down the path with the cameras behind them. But before Wade could follow them, Fox reached out and grabbed his shoulder. "So, what's up with this family?"

A line formed between Wade's eyes. "What do you mean?"

He was Eli's best friend, but that didn't mean he

knew Audrey's family very well. He'd always thought Audrey was really cool, but he'd been caught off guard by her kid sister. And it seemed like Mrs. Hudson was just as prone to drama.

Fox sighed. "Is everyone so high strung all the time?"

Wade chuckled and put his arm around Fox's shoulder. "Maybe if you didn't spend all your time scraping barnacles off the bottom of boats, you would know."

"That's not what I do, and you know that," Fox said, barely resisting the urge to roll his eyes at Wade. "I'm a motorboat mechanic."

"Fine, you scrape barnacles off of motors, then." Wade gave Fox's shoulder a shove. "And I'd be high strung too if I'd been through what Mrs. Hudson has. Her husband left her with four young children and an empty bank account. Milo disappeared off to who knows where. Now she's about to celebrate her first daughter's marriage on television. I think she's allowed to be a little...excitable."

"You're right," Fox said and turned his eyes up to the canopy of leaves above his head. He'd heard Audrey talk a little about her family, but hearing about it and seeing it in person were two different things.

A heavy sigh escaped Fox's lips. Wade made some excellent points that made him reconsider his flash judgements on Mrs. Hudson, but that still left Sienna and her annoying tendencies. Whatever her past, Fox was still worried she might ruin things for everyone. Girls who wanted attention that much usually got it, no matter who they hurt in the process.

"I'm always right." Wade smacked Fox's back. "Now, let's go meet this couple and get it over with."

## FIVE

## 10 Days Until Dream Wedding

---

SIENNA KNEW she needed to tone down the theatrics.

Her sisters loved her, but they had their limits, and Audrey's was fast approaching. Sienna could tell from the way the corner of her mouth was curled down. And Harper...well, Sienna didn't know what was up with Harper, but she'd been out of it since this morning.

Maybe Harper was worried about her bakery. It was just a quick drive down the mountain into town, but the filming schedule didn't allow for long breaks. It would make sense if that was the reason she was distracted, except Harper wasn't on her phone calling or texting her business partner. She just kept staring off in the direction of the crew's tent.

"Hey, I'm sure the food will be good, don't worry," said Sienna, coming to put an arm around Harper's shoulder. They were outside the dining room, waiting to go in. "I know you have strict criteria, but you'll only have to eat it for ten days."

Harper looked at her, eyes wide. She shook her

head, then smiled. "Yeah, you're probably used to crappy craft services, huh, you big movie star?"

Sienna's stomach dropped when she saw Audrey's lip curl down even further.

"Look, I know I've been a little over the top, and I'm sorry," Sienna said.

Audrey didn't look at her, but at least she stopped frowning.

"This is your big thing, I know," Sienna continued. "But it could be big for me too."

It could save more than just her career, but she didn't want to get into details right now. Their mother was nearby, and she was the last person Sienna wanted to know about all the trouble that waited for her back in New York when this was over.

*No, there will be no trouble*, Sienna told herself. She was going to make an impression on Bruce and Jason and get her name and face in front of the right people. She would have actual roles that paid money. No more double shifts at the café just to make rent. Her life would be everything she wanted it to be.

But not at the expense of her big sister.

"Just let me know if I'm too much, okay?" asked Sienna. "Don't do that worried lip thing. It makes me crazy."

At this, Audrey gave her a small smile. "Fine. I'll let you know."

Just then, Jason Castle appeared, made up and suited in a way that almost hid his age. He'd been playing a teenager when Sienna was a kid, but there was no way he was less than forty.

Sienna felt a little better that it wasn't just women in show business who felt the pressure to look young forever, until the familiar fear kicked in that she only had a few years left until she'd be considered too old for most roles. She had to make her mark *now*, before it was too late.

"Just a quick check in about tonight," said Jason, his white smile flashing at them all. "Cocktail hour is just to get some shots of you all mingling. Let's see some of the bride's team chatting with the groom's team. Interact with the hotel staff. Feel free to even come up to me." He laughed, but no one else did.

*Awk*-ward. Sienna caught Audrey's eye and bit her lip to keep from smiling.

"We won't be giving you mic packs, so we won't catch individual conversations. This could be a good time to think about who will be team leads."

Sienna's ears perked up.

"It can be the maid of honor and best man, but it doesn't have to be. You know in reality TV we like surprises. At the end, I'll ask who will step forward to lead each team."

Sienna had her hand on Audrey's arm and squeezed tight.

This was how she could rise above the reality TV stereotype. Treating the role of team lead like an actual role would be a great way to show off her abilities. She would be encouraging when needed, heartbroken if they lost a challenge, and sneaky while also lovable when strategizing.

It was perfect.

Now she just had to convince the others it was a good idea.

———

FOX DID NOT LIKE MINGLING. He gripped the cup in his hand like it was a lifeline. As he made small talk with the owner of the hotel, Alex, and his wife, Willa, he tried to keep his eyes from wandering over to where Sienna stood with her sisters and Reagan.

Sienna was talking animatedly and waving her arms around, and the other three girls looked at her with frowns. Whatever she was so excited about, they were not on board.

*Probably just something to draw the camera's attention.*

"Alright, alright, let's keep mingling!" Jason was moving around the room talking to the small groups of people, leading certain people toward each other to make it look like there was more activity than there really was.

Fox was pleasantly surprised to find out that Alex and Willa were down to earth people, and not the snobby business types he'd been expecting. So, when they, along with their staff, were asked to participate in tonight's shoot, Fox had been relieved. Their presence made this whole thing a little more bearable. Fox still couldn't believe this kind of farce was what Audrey and Eli wanted, but here he was. And somehow Eli had convinced him to be team leader for the guys. Something about it being his duty as best man to do whatever Eli wanted.

Fox did not remember a clause about that…

"Here, why don't you come stand next to this handsome fellow." Jason led Sienna right toward Fox. "His dark hair with your blonde will look great on camera."

Sienna beamed up at Jason, and Fox fought the urge to gag. Not something he wanted caught on camera.

"Trying to get on his good side?" Fox murmured as the older actor floated off to pair up more people.

"Of course, why wouldn't I?" She looked genuinely surprised. Or maybe she was just that good of an actor.

"He's a has-been."

"He has connections."

Fox snorted. "To who? The guild for reality show hosts?"

"Why do you care? It's not your career."

No, it wasn't. But someone needed to set her straight. "It's important not to attach yourself to the wrong people early on."

She narrowed her eyes, and Fox's heart sped up a bit.

"At least, that's what I hear," he said quickly, running a hand through his hair. "From those in the biz."

"And what is it that you do, exactly, that makes you so familiar with 'the biz'?"

He cleared his throat. "I work on boats."

Her eyes lit up. "Like a performer on cruise ships?"

Fox tried not to laugh. Performing on a cruise ship sounded like the worst kind of hell. Trapped on the water, no thank you. "Like, I repair boats. Motors, technically. A motor mechanic."

"Oh." Her brow furrowed. In the brief space of her judging silence, the buzz of voices around them filled Fox's ears.

*It shouldn't matter what she thinks.*

Finally, she looked up at him. "That sounds...interesting."

"Sorry to disappoint. Nothing to be gained from talking to me."

She shook her head. "That's not what I meant. It's

only, you seem so…" She tilted her head to one side. "In control of your body." She flushed. "I mean, in a way that I've only seen in other performers. Not what I'd expect from a motor mechanic."

He cocked an eyebrow. "And you know many motor mechanics in New York, do you?"

She flushed again. "Well, no. I mostly know other actors."

"You mean waiter-slash-actors?"

She glared at him. "Is it really necessary to be mean?"

He held up his hands. "Hey, you started it."

"What?" Her voice was an octave higher, and she shoved a finger into his chest. "I did no such thing. You were talking about Jason and—" She stopped herself when she realized they were drawing the attention of others in the room—and Bruce, who had shown up at some point, in a different suit than this morning.

She cleared her throat and took a step back. "Look, I'm sorry if I offended you. Just now and, ah, earlier today."

Fox's eyebrows shot up so high they nearly flew off his face. "Did you seriously just apologize?"

"And are you seriously this mean to everyone?"

He wasn't, but something about her brought out the teasing schoolboy in him. "Hey, I am who I am. No hiding behind a fake persona just for attention."

Her cheeks turned a bright crimson. "That's not what actors do. They bring characters to life, whether it's on stage or in front of the camera. I love getting to do that. It has nothing to do with attention."

Fox snorted again. "An actor who hates attention. That's a new one."

"I never said I hated it. Just that's not what I love most about what I do." She looked at him closely. "What do you love about your job?"

Ugh, had she somehow talked to Eli and decided to gang up on him tonight? Why did everyone want him to love his job?

He shrugged. "It's a job. I like the money it pays me."

*And that it has nothing to do with my old life.*

"And that's what you've always wanted to do? Work on boat motors?"

"Actually, I hate the water." Why was he telling her this? It must be those deep blue eyes. It was like they were staring into his soul. He glanced around the room for someone to save him, but everyone was involved in their own conversations.

She crossed her arms. "Interesting. Sounds like I'm not the only one hiding behind a fake persona. You're just too stubborn to admit it."

This woman was infuriating. How was it possible for her to be so attractive yet so repellent at the same time?

"Wow, feeling a lot of tension here."

Fox cringed as he heard Bruce behind him.

The producer placed a hand on Fox's shoulder, and he tried not to back away. "This is great, the bride's team versus the groom's team, exactly what we want."

Sienna smiled at Bruce, a slightly different one than she'd given Jason. This one was more desperate. "Whatever you need, just let me know. I'm actually an actor in New York."

"Oh, right, I think one of the production assistants mentioned that." Bruce frowned as he looked her up and down. "Well, stick close to this guy, you're a dream to film together. I couldn't write better tension if I tried —not that reality TV is ever scripted." He chuckled and gave them a wink before walking over to Jason.

Fox turned to Sienna. "No."

Her mouth dropped open. "I didn't even say anything."

"I can see it written all over your face. I'm not playing into whatever he has planned. I'm here for Audrey and Eli."

"So am I." She put her hands on her hips and glared at him. "Don't even try to pull the 'I love them more' card. You'll lose."

"Just stay away from me when filming. I'm not here to be a star. Don't drag me into something I don't want."

She pursed her lips, looking furious, and flounced off to where Audrey was standing with her mom. Fox breathed a sigh of relief. The further away he could stay from her over the next week and a half, the better.

"Alright, alright, the time has come." Everyone stopped their chatting and turned to where Jason was standing at the head of the room. "It's time to meet our team leads. These two will be in charge of strategy and coordination of their team's attempts in each challenge. It's a big role, so I hope the bride and groom have chosen wisely."

Ugh, Fox had forgotten all about this part thanks to his bickering with Sienna.

"Will the team lead for the groom's team please come forward."

So much for not being a star.

Fox cast a withering glance in Eli's direction and made his way next to Jason. He tried his best to ignore the cameras pointed right at him from the back of the room. It was the same set up as this morning, but it made it worse to know exactly where they were.

"And now will the team lead for the bride's team join me?"

Fox had his eyes on Reagan, but she didn't move. A flicker of movement from the other direction caught his eye, and he knew without turning his head who it would be. Fox took in her fake smile and let out a heavy sigh. Of course, it would be her.

"Sienna, Fox, please face each other."

They did, Fox suppressing a groan the entire time.

"Now shake hands."

Her hand flew out straight, the smile never wavering on her perfect face. She had her Hollywood makeup on again, and her extra shiny hair was enormously distracting.

And not at all attractive.

Nope, not at all.

Fox ignored the way his heart sped up when his and Sienna's hands met. They shook twice, and Jason announced, "Let the games begin."

SIX

## 9 Days Until Dream Wedding

THE SUN STREAMING through Sienna's window was brighter than it was in New York. Maybe because she was in a hotel room twice the size of her entire apartment, and it wasn't in the basement. Or maybe it was because she couldn't remember the last time she hadn't had to set her alarm to go off before the sun went up.

With a jolt, she sat upright in the silky cotton sheets. Sun meant it was morning, which meant she was going to be late.

Again.

She'd meant to wake up early and go for a run, but the early flight and full day of filming yesterday must have taken more out of her than she realized. Then she'd been up half the night thinking about Fox.

She'd never met someone who seemed completely oblivious to how insanely good-looking he was. Half the guys she knew in New York spent three hours a day at the gym trying to get a body like his. And that just slightly-too-long hair would cost a boatload at a fancy

49

salon. Speaking of boats, there was no way that's all he did. Fox was a mystery.

Even more mysterious was why someone she'd just met would talk to her like that. She'd apologized and everything. Sure, not everyone liked her right away, but no man had ever hated her the way he seemed to. What was his problem? She wanted the same thing he did: a gorgeous wedding for Audrey and Eli. But if she could help her career at the same time, why should she feel bad about that?

With a mumbled curse she threw on one of her cuter pairs of leggings and added an oversized tank from her alma mater, Carter College. She swept her hair up into a messy ponytail high on her head, and dabbed concealer on the worst of her imperfections.

She put a hand on her hip and turned back and forth in front of the full-length mirror on the back of the bathroom door, pleased with what she saw.

It was the perfect amount of "I just woke up like this" but polished enough that it would look good if there was no time for makeup before the first shoot of the day.

Sienna rushed out the door and down the hallway but nearly collided with someone at the top of the stairs.

"Watch it," said the now-familiar voice of Fox. "You really don't pay attention to anyone other than yourself, do you?"

She barely had time to register his sweaty face and athletic gear before he pushed past her and headed to his room. Had he been for a run? Were those biceps revealed by his sleeveless shirt for real? Wait, *what* had he just said to her?

He'd totally overreacted to accidentally bumping

into someone. He must be grumpy about something, but that seemed like Fox's default mood.

After staring down the hall for a minute too long, Sienna realized if he wasn't downstairs yet, then she couldn't be *that* late. She hurried down the stairs and into the dining room, grabbed a muffin, and took a seat in between Harper and Reagan. "Any idea what we'll be doing today?" she asked.

Harper shook her head. "They want authentic reactions to whatever announcements they have."

Reagan sighed. "It's a little distracting, having all these cameras everywhere."

"Just pretend it's a person," Sienna said, biting into her muffin.

"More like a million people." Reagan shuddered. "And they're all just waiting for you to do something embarrassing."

"Girls," her mother hissed from her spot behind them.

*Why was she even here?*

Bruce had made it clear that the parents of the bride and groom weren't required to show up to any of the competitions. Eli's parents had taken this to heart and were nowhere to be found in the large dining room. But of course, Sienna's mother had to be seen, and she'd been sighing loudly ever since Sienna walked in. Not only that, Sienna could practically feel her mother's eyes boring into the back of her skull every time she spoke.

She turned around and gave her a sickly-sweet smile. "Good morning, Mother."

"They're going to start any minute. You need to be paying attention."

Sienna looked around the room. Everyone was

talking—the bridesmaids, groomsmen, even the production crew. The only person not chatting it up with anyone else was their mother, who sat up straight with her hands folded demurely in her lap.

When she turned back around, Reagan's face looked pale, and she was biting her nails.

Sienna gently pulled Reagan's hand from her mouth before she chewed her fingers down to stubs. "Be on your best cotillion behavior," Sienna said.

Reagan groaned. "I thought I was done with those days."

Sienna shook her head.

When Audrey had brought home her new friend Reagan from college, twelve-year-old Sienna had been mesmerized by her beauty queen looks and super polite manners. Reagan had stepped into the gaping hole Milo had left in their family and filled it with sweet tea and the best stories about all the scandals from her all-girls boarding school.

In an effort to distract the unofficial fourth sister to the Hudson girls, Sienna asked Reagan to tell the story of when she and her roommate snuck over to the all-boys prep school. Sienna has heard it at least a hundred times, but it felt like being home, and made everyone temporarily forget all about *Wedding Games*.

At least, until Jason Castle came into the room. "Good morning, wedding party," he said with his patented bright smile on his face. "Is everyone ready for the first competition?"

Sienna sat up straight in her seat, ready to show Jason—and her mom—she was all business. She answered with a loud "yeah" but was the only one. She glanced around the room and realized that everyone was looking at her—Reagan and her sisters with patient smiles, and the groomsmen with amusement.

Well, all of the groomsmen except for Fox. The scowl affixed to his face felt as much a staple to Fox as the perma-smile was to Jason. And while she couldn't be sure, Sienna swore he even rolled his eyes at her just before turning his head in the opposite direction.

Sienna took a deep breath, careful not to let the cameras see how his attitude affected her. While a little friendly competition might help her show off her acting skills, it wouldn't do her any good to lose her cool just because the best man couldn't play nice.

She smiled and turned back to where Jason was explaining the rules of the first competition. "You'll spend your morning doing a scavenger hunt in down-town Wellspring," he said. "Now, this gives a slight advantage to those who live here, but we've found ways to make it challenging and fun for everyone."

Sienna frowned. As the team leader, she had hoped to excel at every challenge, but looking for things? She didn't know the area very well, not after being in New York for so long.

But Harper's bakery was downtown.

Sienna looked up at her sister, expecting to share a conspiratorial glance, but Harper was staring out the window. She probably knew the area better than anyone else, if only she would get her head in the game.

"There are five items scattered around the shops and surrounding areas. The first team to find all five will get to choose the flowers for the entire ceremony, including the bride's bouquet."

*Okay*, Sienna thought. While the flowers weren't the most important aspect of the wedding day—not like the food or the cake—they could make or break how Audrey looked in her wedding album.

She tried to imagine what the guys would choose if they won. She wouldn't put it past Mr. McGrumperson to convince Eli to go with something utilitarian like plain, white carnations.

At least if the girls won, Sienna could ensure the flowers were bright and full of life. Just like Audrey and —usually—Harper.

And win was just what she planned to do with, or without, Harper's help.

———

FIVE HOURS into the scavenger hunt, Fox had decided he'd had enough for one day. At least having the bridesmaids and the groomsmen running around downtown looking for different things meant the guys hadn't seen the girls very much today. Which suited Fox just fine.

Unfortunately, it did mean the cameras had been there for every agonizing second of the day. They caught the moment Fox tripped over an upturned part of the sidewalk in his hurry to find the next item, and he was sure they zoomed in on his face when Sienna and her team found the handmade firefly lamp before the groomsmen.

And even though Eli had said he didn't care about the flowers, and Fox had sworn to himself that he wouldn't turn into a competitive jerk, the sight of Sienna and her triumphant smile at the small victory of beating the guys to the lamp, made him want to win the competition anyway.

But they didn't.

And when Jason Castle broke the news that the bridesmaids had arrived at the final destination with the last item just minutes before the groomsmen, Fox couldn't help letting out a frustrated groan that he was sure Bruce would adore.

He wasn't sure how he would survive nine more days of this.

So, the second the cameraman switched it off and Austin, the production assistant they'd been assigned for the day, told them they were all set, Fox practically ran to the coffee shop to escape the stress of the day and grab a pick me up. It was the only break they'd been given in the schedule to go off the inn's property, and Fox wasn't about to waste it.

He felt a little guilty for not going to Harper's Flour Girl Bakery, but the coffee was ten times better at The Brew House. Besides, Fox couldn't be sure there wouldn't be cameras at the bakery getting filler shots or interviewing the staff or something.

Just as he sat down with his large, black coffee and took his first sip, *she* walked through the door.

In her hand was a small, golden statue of a bride and groom that looked a lot like a cake topper. "Oh, hey there, loser," she said in a teasing tone as she walked over to his table.

Fox looked around the coffee shop to make sure they were truly off camera before saying, "Like I care who won."

The smile on Sienna's face fell, and without waiting for an invitation, she took the seat across from him.

"Please, won't you join me?" Fox said with a tight-lipped smile.

His sarcasm was completely lost on Sienna. That, or

she chose to ignore it, because she didn't move. "You should."

He looked up at her. "I should what?"

Sienna let out a dramatic sigh. "You should care who won. You're Eli's best man, and it's kind of your job to make sure that he and my sister get a decent wedding when all of this is said and done."

"Well, with a little sister who obviously cares so much for the outcome…"

A line formed between Sienna's brows. "What's that supposed to mean?"

"Nothing. I'm sure your reasons for smiling at every camera are altruistic."

"You're mad because I'm enjoying this?"

Fox raised an eyebrow. "Enjoying it or using it to your professional advantage?"

She set her trophy on the table and crossed her arms. "I get to spend ten days with my sisters, I get to see Audrey and Eli get married, and yeah, I get to spend some time in front of the camera." She closed her eyes and shook her head. "I'm not going to feel guilty for having fun while I do my job."

Fox grunted.

"And if you took a few minutes to pull out whatever stick you have hiding up your butt, you might find out that life isn't meant to be approached with a scowl and a bad attitude."

Caught between a laugh and a grunt, Fox stared at the tiny blonde annoyance sitting across from him. It wasn't that he didn't want to enjoy life—or have fun. He'd just seen too much. Experienced too much. And if something felt too good to be true, then it probably was.

Of course, Sienna was too young and naive to

understand that. She still lived in the delusional world that acting gigs would fall in her lap, and her career would be all fun and games

But it wasn't his job to tell her that. She'd learn it eventually, and painfully, on her own. He should just stay away from her, though he wasn't sure how possible that would be while confined to a tiny mountainside inn.

Though she did have a good point about making more effort for Eli. It wasn't just enough to be here for his best friend, Fox needed to put in actual effort into *Wedding Games*.

Not that he would ever admit that to Sienna.

"Just worry about your own attitude," he said and stood up. His few minutes of calm had been ruined so he might as well go back to his room at the inn.

"I don't need to," she said, flipping her hair over her shoulder. "We're winning."

Fox stormed out the door with his coffee, almost able to ignore the way the afternoon light hit her golden waves.

## SEVEN

## 8 Days Until Dream Wedding

---

THE NEXT MORNING, Sienna was still riding the high of winning. With one competition down, there were still four more to go. But she was in it to win it—even with these early mornings. Really, whoever thought they needed to get started at 8 a.m. every day was clearly a guy who didn't require more than a quick shower to look camera ready.

Regardless, Sienna planned to bring a hundred-and-ten percent to the next challenge and show everyone she was a valuable asset. She would make the connections she needed to ensure her big break was right around the corner, she would give Audrey and Eli the wedding of their dreams, and she would do it all while teaching Fox it was okay to enjoy life every once in a while.

Though she doubted he could manage a second of joy even if his life depended on it.

Sienna was still irritated at his lack of enthusiasm during her run-in with him at The Brew House. Why had Eli chosen him as best man if he didn't even care? Audrey seemed to love Fox too. There was something she was missing, and Sienna hated being the last to know.

Just thinking about it made her head hurt.

Or more likely it was the lack of caffeine in her body.

Sienna knew she had just enough time to grab some java before going to the meeting room to hear about that day's competition. She hurried down the stairs and was surprised to see her mom. Audrey had reminded her the previous night that she could enjoy the inn's spa services instead of showing up to all of the meetings and competitions.

"Aren't you supposed to be in the meeting room already?"

Yeesh. How did her mom manage to know the schedule despite not being a part of the events? Sienna smiled. "I have five minutes. It's okay."

Her mother shook her head. "Has all your time in New York made you forget everything I taught you?"

"I haven't forgotten. Five minutes early is on time, on time is late, and late is unacceptable," Sienna recited. The words had been ingrained in her mind for as long as she could remember. At least it meant she'd never been late to an audition.

"Exactly," said her mother. "So why is it that every time I see you, you're running late?"

"I'm not."

"I think you're developing bad habits up there. Maybe it's time to come home."

*This again?* Sienna rolled her eyes. "I told you, I'm not ready to come home yet. I have a life there."

"Sienna, you're twenty-three years old, and you still

don't have a steady income. It may be time to start considering different career paths."

"But acting is important to me. I want to make sure I give it everything I have. And I work three different jobs to afford life there, so you don't have to worry about me." Though *afford* was stretching the truth a little bit.

"But I do worry." Her mom's face turned serious. "And besides, sometimes you can give it everything you have, and it's still not enough."

"Mother." Sienna reached out for her mother's shoulder. Next would be the long list of everything her mother had given up for them. Sienna didn't have time for that or she really would be late.

"I love you girls, and I'm thankful you've never gone hungry. But do you know how much I hate that Audrey is going through all of this just to get married? It's awful."

Sienna shrugged. "She doesn't seem to mind."

"Maybe, maybe not. Regardless, this is about her. I want to see you on your best behavior while we're here. Give it everything you've got, without going overboard. And for the love of everything, don't be late to anything else."

"I'm always on my best behavior, I want to give it my all, which is why I'm grabbing coffee first." Sienna leaned in and kissed her mother's cheek. "And I promise not to be late."

Sienna waved a quick goodbye over her shoulder and walked to the dining room. But as soon as she turned the corner, Fox stepped into view. In his hand was the biggest coffee thermos Sienna had ever seen— and she'd pulled quite a few all-nighters in college.

"They're about to start in the meeting room," he

said, barely making eye-contact with her before he stormed off.

"*They're about to start in the meeting room,*" she mimicked under her breath. Was everyone going to comment on her punctuality today? She'd be there just as soon as she got some coffee. And she wouldn't be late.

Sienna grabbed a small paper cup and the stainless-steel carafe from the table, but when she tipped the container, nothing came out. Her lips turned down as she pressed the release valve on the handle and tipped the carafe for a second time.

Again, nothing.

Sienna took a deep breath as she set it down and unscrewed the lid. When she looked inside, it was completely empty. Not a single drop of the liquid gold remained. She crumpled the paper cup and tossed it on the counter. "Ugh."

"Ugh, is right."

The voice startled Sienna, and she quickly turned to see the head chef standing there with hands on her hips. The embroidery on her uniform read "Marcey." Sienna had seen the woman a few times since arriving at the Emerald Inn, usually at mealtimes chatting with the owners of the inn. And while she was also pretty young, the look she gave Sienna was as scary as anything Grandma Hudson had given her when she tried to steal an extra cookie from the jar.

Marcey pointed a finger at Sienna. "You may be here filming this reality TV show, but that doesn't mean you can leave trash all over my dining room."

If Sienna wasn't so disappointed from finding the carafe empty, she might have apologized instead of asking, "Do you have any more coffee?"

Marcey fixed her with a stare, and Sienna knew she'd pushed too far.

"Fine," she said and grabbed the paper cup from the table. She threw it in the trash can on her way out the door.

Apparently, Fox wasn't the only grumpy person around here.

But he *was* the one who had just ruined her morning. He'd taken the last of the coffee in his giant man mug and gotten Sienna in trouble with the person in charge of providing more coffee.

Sienna couldn't wait to teach him a lesson by winning. Again.

---

WHY WAS it every time Fox tried to enjoy a nice cup of coffee, Sienna showed up?

It wasn't enough that she was on the verge of ruining the entire show for Eli and Audrey, but she had to ruin every moment in between with her plastic smile and desire to be in front of the cameras.

She was going to be late to that morning's meeting, and then had the audacity to mock him the second he turned the corner. He'd left the room, not gone deaf.

How immature and self-centered could a person be?

Fox looked down at his watch and saw that he would be cutting it close if he wasn't careful, and he wasn't about to stoop to her level. He picked up his pace and hurried inside the meeting room.

"Who spit in your coffee?" Wade asked.

Fox flopped down in a chair at the groomsmen's

table. "Sienna," he said, before he could think twice about it.

Wade and Eli chuckled.

"Obviously, she didn't *actually* spit in my coffee."

"Obviously." Eli rolled his eyes.

"But she made fun of me in the dining hall."

Wade gasped loudly and put a hand to his chest. "She didn't!"

Fox felt heat creep up his neck.

"Do you want me to call her mom and tell her what a meanie she was to you?" Eli put a comforting hand on Fox's shoulder, but his face was beat red from holding in a laugh.

Fox slumped back in his seat. "Very funny," he mumbled.

"No," Wade said, his face still serious. "Fox's dreamy eyes having zero effect on a girl is no laughing matter."

"And neither is that sad excuse for a goatee you have going on," Fox said.

Wade's loud laugh caused some of the crew to look in their direction. "You wish you looked this good with a beard."

Fox rolled his eyes. As if that monstrosity could be considered a beard. "So, what do you think we're going to do today?"

Eli lifted the bright orange shirt in front of him. "Let's hope it's not a paint gun battle, because this is going to be impossible to hide in these eyesores."

"Not to mention the bruises and welts that would come from something like that," Wade said.

"And I doubt Bruce is that ruthless," Fox said. "They may want drama, but a bride with bruises isn't a great image for *Wedding Games,* no matter how they'd want to spin it."

"Okay, so no paintball," Eli said, looking down at the shirt today. "But it looks like it's sponsored by that protein bar you're always eating, Wade."

Wade's cheeks turned red. "There's nothing wrong with wanting to be healthy."

"What's their slogan again?" Eli snapped his fingers. "Power to be brave."

"Every day," Wade muttered.

"That's right," Fox said. "I hope we don't have to do something brave but stupid today like jump off a mountain."

"Think there's any leftover bravery left in Wade from when he lived off these things?" Eli playfully elbowed Wade, who smacked his arm away.

"You guys are a riot." Now it was Wade's turn to slump in his seat, the curious eyes of the others in the dining hall glancing over at their table.

"That doesn't sound like a brave attitude to me," Fox said, relishing the way they could slip back into this playful banter.

It was something he'd told himself he didn't miss when he was in Kitty Hawk, and it had been easy to keep telling himself the lie when his best friend was seven hours away. But now that he was back in Wellspring, sitting with Wade and Eli, he could see how flimsy the veil he'd pulled over his eyes really was.

"Well, regardless, if a protein bar sponsored the next event, then it's safe to assume it's something physical, right?" Fox asked.

Eli shrugged. "Probably."

"And as much as you want to make fun of me for

bulking up, these muscles are going to come in handy." Wade flexed his biceps, causing the tattoos to dance.

It was a parlor trick that Wade had practiced time and time again, wanting to impress the ladies. Fox rolled his eyes just as Harry slid into the seat next to him.

According to the clock on the wall, it was 8:01 and Jason was just now getting his mic queued up. Apparently, Sienna wasn't the only one who didn't take this show seriously. Fox resisted the urge to chide Harry for his tardiness and looked over at the bridesmaids' table only to notice that Sienna was still missing.

Did that girl care about anyone other than herself? Doubtful.

"Alright, alright," Jason said, his voice booming through the room. "It's time to introduce the second competition. Today contestants will be showing how brave they are by tackling the *Wedding Games* obstacle course, sponsored in part by—"

The door leading into the meeting room squeaked, and in walked Sienna. Her eyes went wide, and she stopped dead in her tracks when she realized she had interrupted Jason. But her look of surprise was quickly replaced by a serene smile.

"Sorry, I'm late," she said with a small wave, like the whole world revolved around her.

Fox couldn't hide his irritation as effortlessly as Sienna masked her initial shock, and his angry gaze followed her as she sat down beside her sisters. Audrey gave Sienna a disapproving frown, but neither Reagan nor Harper said, or did, anything.

Bruce walked over to where a confused Jason stood.

"Let's start from the top," Bruce said and waved his hand above his head.

Bruce sent a glare Sienna's direction before he stepped out of the shot. Fox's stomach twisted into knots. She'd destroy this whole show if she wasn't careful.

And Fox was determined not to let that happen.

## 8 Days Until Dream Wedding

---

AFTER WALKING into the meeting room late and listening to Jason Castle go over the rules for the next competition, Sienna trudged her way behind Harper to the giant field that was half a mile from the inn. Today's winning team got to choose the music, and Fox would probably choose something depressing like *The Funeral March.*

Sienna *had* to win.

Reagan crossed her arms nervously when they saw what was waiting for them. "This looks like something straight out of basic training."

"Or one of those races you pay a ton of money for, just to prove just how tough you are," said Harper, looking equally anxious.

*"Oh, look at me, I can run in the mud, and climb a wall, and jump over fire. I'm so amazing."* Sienna used her tough guy voice and was pleased to see it made the girls laugh.

Though secretly, Sienna had always wondered what it would be like to run in a race like that. And now, it looked like she was going to have her chance.

Jason Castle was standing off to the side, still wearing a perfectly tailored suit, while everyone else had been given the opportunity to change into more comfortable clothing. This event was sponsored by some protein bar company, and each contestant was wearing a shirt with the logo plastered on the front and back.

Sienna hated the stupid thing. But bright orange wasn't flattering on anyone so she wouldn't be the only one looking washed out during today's filming. Her eyes scanned the crowd until they landed on Fox, who didn't look terrible in today's uniform.

It wasn't fair that someone so grouchy could look so good in such an awful color.

"We'll let the winning team from our first competition choose who gets first stab at the obstacle course," Jason said, breaking Sienna's train of thought.

The four girls huddled together in a small circle.

"I say we go first," Audrey said first. "It's still cool enough that we might not get super sweaty."

That wasn't a bad way of looking at it. The Hudson sisters all had pale skin that turned bright red when they did any kind of physical exertion. Reagan, the redhead, was even paler. If they went first, they would look good for the camera.

"Harper?" Sienna asked, turning her head to face her other sister.

"Huh?"

Sienna suppressed a sigh. She wasn't sure what was up with Harper, but whatever it was, she needed to get her head in the game, like, yesterday. "I was wondering if you'd like to go first or second for this competition."

"Oh." Harper bit her bottom lip. "Whatever."

This time, Sienna did sigh. She turned to Reagan. "What about you?"

Reagan's mouth curved into a sly smile. "Well, I was thinking we could let the guys go first."

Audrey's head snapped in her best friend's direction, mock betrayal written all over her face. "As maid of honor, are you even allowed to disagree with me?"

Reagan rolled her eyes. "Hear me out. The guys are going to think they have this one in the bag, right? It's a physical test, and I bet they're all talking about how strong and manly they are right now."

The girls all looked over to Eli and his groomsmen. Wade said something that made the other guys laugh, and he pulled up his sleeve and flexed a tattooed bicep.

Sienna started to laugh when she saw Fox doing the same. Even though he was slightly shorter and less stocky than Wade, that bicep was nothing to laugh about. Fox was made of muscles in all the right places.

"Well," Reagan continued. "I bet they've all underestimated how hard we've worked to look good in our dresses. Audrey, you've been in the weight room four times a week for the last month to make sure your arms look amazing in your strapless dress."

Audrey nodded.

"And Sienna." Reagan gave her a smile. "You're always making sure you're in shape for whatever role might come your way, right?"

"Of course." No expensive gym membership required when you spent your days running heavy trays back and forth from the kitchen.

"So, if we let the guys go first, they may underestimate us. And it's possible we can surprise them with how well we do."

"Oh, I like the way you think." Sienna's smile grew. "Then it's decided, we'll go second."

The four girls broke apart and turned to face an expectant-looking Jason Castle.

"Have you decided?" he asked.

Sienna stood up straight, and after a brief, but dramatic pause, she answered. "We're going to let the groomsmen go first."

All the guys started bumping fists with one another. Wade went so far as to pound his chest in an over-the-top macho display. Harry stood off to the side, however, looking a little bewildered. Or maybe just bored.

At least Fox seemed to have changed his tune and was finally taking things seriously. He flexed his arms above his head and then ran in place.

"Alright, alright," Jason said to the guys. "You heard the ladies, you're up first. You'll start off with the tire run, climb over the wall, swing from the monkey bars over the mud pit, army crawl under our rope course, jump from trunk to trunk in our stepping stone area, and then sprint to the bell at the opposite end of the field. We'll be taking an average of everyone's times, so there's no need to show off in this one. You're only as strong as your weakest link."

Sienna smiled triumphantly as Harry continued to pout off to the side. She wasn't sure what Reagan saw in the guy, but right now, she was happy he was the third groomsman. The moody peacock was sure to slow down their average.

"On your mark, get set, go!"

The guys started running. The first obstacle was the tire run. It consisted of about twenty tires tied together, flat on their sides. It seemed simple enough, and the guys all made it through the obstacle without a hitch.

After that, it was the climbing wall. It was tall and had several ropes hanging down the side for people to use to get over. Fox was the first one to the wall, and he immediately grabbed the rope and started climbing. His sleeves were still rolled up, and Sienna could see his muscles bulging from the effort of climbing up.

She couldn't decide if she should be happy that Fox was making an effort after her little pep-talk yesterday, or be upset that she was now in danger of losing.

Wade beat Fox over the wall by a second, with Eli close behind. Who knew teachers were so buff? Even Harry was only a few seconds behind the rest of the guys as they ran over to the monkey bars.

"Come on, babe," Audrey yelled from beside Sienna. "You got this!"

Sienna smacked her sister on the arm. "Don't cheer him on," she said through gritted teeth.

Audrey looked toward her with an unapologetic smile and shrugged her shoulders. "What? He's still my fiancé, and I want him to do well."

"But we don't want them to win." Sienna rolled her eyes.

"Wanna hear a secret?" Audrey leaned in toward Sienna. "I really don't care. As long as I get to marry him in eight days, they can play *Chopsticks* as I walk down the aisle for all I care."

Sienna shook her head and turned her attention back to the obstacle course. Wade and Fox were hurrying across the monkey bars and...wait. Were they trying to knock each other off? What idiots. At least if they succeeded, that would give the bridesmaids an advantage.

She watched them play around for another moment, before her eyes went to where Harry stood hesitating at the edge of the mud pit.

"What is he doing?" Sienna asked under her breath.

Reagan sighed. "His phone."

Sienna turned toward Reagan and raised her brows.

"He's afraid of falling into the mud and ruining it."

"Why doesn't he just set it down?" Audrey asked.

"You don't understand the relationship he was with that thing," Reagan said before she ran over to where Harry stood, his face red.

While Sienna was too far to hear what was being said, the way Reagan frowned probably wasn't a good sign. She didn't know Reagan's fiancé that well, but she'd seen enough entitled jerks in New York to spot one a mile away. Harry slammed the phone into her hand and wiped his hands on his athletic shorts. Then he jumped up and grabbed the monkey bars.

Harry had only made it halfway, when his grip faltered, and he fell into the mud. Sienna laughed, until she saw the murderous look on Harry's face when he stood up. He said something to Reagan that had her rushing back to where the rest of the girls stood.

"Are you——"

"I'm fine," Reagan answered quickly and turned to gaze back to where the guys were still competing.

Wade and Fox still led the pack as they finished the army crawl and jogged over to where tree trunks of various heights were scattered. They started jumping from trunk to truck, with Eli still close behind.

Sienna looked at Harry just in time to see him shake

his head and get down on his stomach for the army crawl. Moments earlier, she'd been happy to see him lagging behind, but after watching him speak to Reagan the way he did, the victory felt hollow.

*Ding! Ding! Ding!*

Wade rang the bell wildly until Fox caught up and pushed him out of the way. He, too, rang the bell enthusiastically. Wade pushed him back, and the two guys started laughing.

Fox was actually *laughing*.

It completely transformed his face. Even as Eli ran up and rang the bell, Sienna couldn't look away from Fox. The sight of him happy had her transfixed. That was, until his gaze found hers. His gorgeous smile dropped, and the familiar scowl fell back into place.

Freed from her trance, Sienna looked away and tried to push down the flutter of disappointment at his reaction. Why did he hate her so much? Okay, so she'd accidentally mistaken him for the janitor that first day, but she'd apologized. And then she'd called him out for not trying hard enough for his best friend, but clearly, he'd listened.

Maybe it was just her. She wasn't enough.

Was she really that surprised someone like him wouldn't like her? He was this gorgeous specimen of a man that even her big sister sounded half in love with when she talked about him. Sienna just wasn't the kind of girl that mattered to people like that. She hadn't been enough to make Dad stay. Or bring Milo back from wherever he'd disappeared to. Or even enough for Fox to be decent to her.

She felt the sting of tears filling her eyes and fought to keep them at bay. She didn't want anyone to see her cry, and especially didn't want it captured for the entire world to see.

The bell rang out again as Harry finally made his way over to where the rest of the guys stood waiting.

Jason Castle called for everyone to gather around him. "The judges are tallying the final scores. Once they're finished, we'll have the time for the bridesmaids to beat. In the meantime, take five."

With that, everyone dispersed.

Sienna decided to take the opportunity to compose herself—something that should have come easily to her since she was an actor. But yesterday had been a long one, and she was operating on zero caffeine, so she needed to find an area away from the cameras to get it together.

She wandered over to a lightly wooded area just off to the field where the obstacle course had been set up. She leaned against the trunk of a fir tree and closed her eyes.

Just because Fox didn't want to smile at her, didn't mean Sienna could start breaking down now. She had to lead the bridesmaids to victory this week. She needed to support her sister. She needed...

To be quiet.

Someone was coming.

Sienna stiffened at the sound of footsteps falling on the twigs and leaves that littered the ground. There was no telling who was walking toward her. With her luck it would be someone with a camera propped over their shoulder. They'd wonder why she was hiding, and then she'd have to lie and say she wasn't.

"Is this far enough from everyone?" asked a female voice that Sienna instantly recognized as Reagan's.

"You don't have to be snippy with me." That was definitely Harry.

*Oh crap. I shouldn't be here.*

Sienna held her breath in an attempt to stay completely silent.

"Snippy? You just told me you're leaving in the middle of the competition. That you won't be here for Eli and Audrey's wedding. How am I supposed to feel right now?"

"Maybe grateful that your fiancé has an incredible job? That way, when we get married, you won't have to go on one of these ridiculous shows to pay for the cake and flowers. You'll be able to get whatever your little heart desires."

A shocked gasp came from Reagan. "Didn't you read the contract? You can't leave before the end."

Sienna pushed herself closer against the trunk at the ruffled sound of movement and snapping twigs.

"Of course I read the contract," Harry said in a deep voice that was almost a growl. "It's my job to read contracts and look for loopholes."

"But—"

"Which means I already know my way out of this one."

Everything went silent, and if it wasn't for the fact that Sienna knew Reagan and Harry were standing just a few feet from where she hid, she'd think she was alone.

"But it'll look really bad," Reagan said, her voice taking on that wavering quality Sienna knew meant tears weren't far behind.

Harry let out a very un-Harry-like snort. "Worse than continuing to be a part of this ridiculous spectacle?

Somehow, I doubt that. Come with me. I can get you out of the contract too."

"But it's my best friend's wedding. I can't just leave." She paused for a second. "And what about Eli? I know you don't know him that well, but he'll be disappointed that you're leaving. They'll be down a groomsman for the competitions. They'll…" Her voice shook and the unmistakable sound of crying rang out through the air.

"Don't cry," Harry said with a sigh. "You'll mess up your makeup."

Reagan sniffled in response.

"Besides, I'm doing this for us," Harry said. "You know my father wants to make me partner. If I take this new case, I'll be one step closer to that goal. And then we can start planning our future, okay?"

"Okay," Reagan said quietly.

"Good girl. Now don't say anything to anyone until I talk to Bruce."

"I'll miss you. Love you."

"Me too. I'll see you back home when this is all over, okay?"

"Yeah, okay."

Sienna let out a long sigh at the sound of footsteps retreating off into the distance.

Thank goodness that was over. She moved from her spot against the tree and came face to face with a very startled Reagan. The older girl's eyes were red-rimmed, and her face pale beneath her makeup.

"H-hey, Sienna." Reagan's eyes darted back and forth. "How long have you been out here?"

Sienna bit her bottom lip and shrugged.

Reagan pushed her lips together. "You heard that then?"

"Yeah." The leaves crunched beneath Sienna's feet as she shifted her weight from side to side. "Want to talk about it?"

Her friend quickly shook her head. "We should get back to the obstacle course. I'm sure they've finished tallying up the times by now."

Sienna kept her mouth closed and walked with Reagan in silence.

But she couldn't help but think that she wouldn't be the only one putting on a brave face during the filming.

## NINE

## 8 Days Until Dream Wedding

Jason Castle called everyone back to the beginning of the course, his perma-smile flashing in the morning sun. Fox wondered if his cheeks ever hurt from the effort of constantly showing every single one of his teeth.

"Alright, alright. The bride's team looks ready to go, but just so you ladies are aware, the groom's team got an excellent time after an impressive show."

"Beat *that*, ladies," Wade said with a grin and something that looked like a football player's touchdown dance.

"We plan to," said Sienna, her blue eyes fierce.

Something in her look made Fox swallow hard. This girl was serious.

And a serious athlete. She whipped through everything at hyper-speed, jumping from the tire run to wall like she was born to do this. Nothing seemed to scare her. She dove headfirst under the rope course and didn't even pause when a nail caught her on the leg. Fox was pretty sure no matter who won, Bruce would be using as much of the footage of Sienna as he could. She looked incredible.

Despite his better judgement, Fox found himself being drawn toward her. His eyes lingered on her as she laughed with her sisters at the finish bell. Somehow, without even realizing what his body was doing, Fox found himself standing at her side.

"That was impressive," he said. When she turned her head and glared at him, he held up his hands. "Really."

A slow smile spread across her face, lighting her up from the inside and making her eyes sparkle.

*Whoa.* The effect her smile had on him was even more unexpected than her performance had been.

"It's all my plastic doll training," she said, her eyes flashing.

And there was the petty brat again.

"Most people with manners would say thank you to a compliment," Fox said, crossing his arms over his chest.

"Thanks for the lesson, Grandpa."

"Grandpa." Fox cleared his throat.

Sienna rolled her eyes. "You're like the grumpy old man on a sitcom, always scowling and grumbling at everyone."

Fox frowned, then caught himself and rearranged his face into something more neutral. "Maybe I just don't feel like smiling like a crazy person anytime a camera is within a two-mile radius of me."

Something passed across her face, too quick for Fox to be sure, but it looked an awful lot like hurt. "At least I'm putting in an actual effort."

"Not this again," Fox grumbled. "That took major effort to get that score."

"You mean the score we're about to beat?"

Fox knew it would be close, and he wasn't willing to admit defeat just yet, so he changed the subject.

"You should probably get that leg looked at before it gangrenes," he said. "Wouldn't want to have to cancel your next JC Penny catalog shoot."

*Okay, that was kind of mean,* he thought as he walked off to rejoin Wade and Eli, but Sienna didn't seem to have even heard him—or she didn't care. She'd already turned her back to him and started talking to her sisters again.

How had Fox gone from wanting to compliment her to insulting her? Sienna was strong and beautiful. And annoyingly perceptive. He *was* kind of like a grumpy grandpa, but he hadn't given up on the world. It was just better for the world if he wasn't such an active participant.

He hadn't always been like this. Once he'd loved being with people, meeting new people, and traveling. But ever since…

Nope, he was *not* going to think about Becky.

He went to stand with Eli and Wade and turned his attention to where the judges were tallying up everyone's times. The girls had been surprisingly fast and agile as they went through the course. The guys exchanged more than a few worried glances that the cameras were sure to have captured.

Finally, Jason Castle reappeared and held a very official-looking paper in his hands. "I have the final results here."

Fox grumbled under his breath. Of all the annoying

things about this experience, having the host narrate everything he did was probably the worst.

"The bride's team put in an impressive performance, with a final average time of ten minutes and forty-three seconds."

Squealing and jumping erupted from the four girls.

"And the groom's team came in at a final average time of…" He paused, looked at his paper, then back up at the camera. "Ten minutes and twelve seconds!"

Sienna and the other girls groaned in unison.

Fox let out a sigh of relief as Wade whooped in joy and started his touchdown dance again. They'd done it. Eli clapped Fox on the back.

"No Avril Lavigne or Black Eyed Peas, I promise," Fox said.

Eli grinned. "Maybe just one. I do have a soft spot for early 2000s pop music, after all."

Fox shook his head and laughed. People did dumb stuff for love, and not just listen to awful music.

"Alright, alright, you've all earned a little break."

Everyone turned to look at Jason Castle.

"Go get cleaned up, and we'll be back here for an afternoon barbecue by the barn."

Fox knew that break wouldn't include a break from the cameras, but at least the hard work was done for the day, and he could focus on hanging out with his friends. And avoiding Sienna.

———

ELI AND FOX were talking to one of the owners of the inn while everyone milled around with plates piled high with ribs and brisket.

"So, Alex, why did you come all the way from Virginia to open up this place?" Eli asked.

Alex started to answer, but Fox's attention was drawn to the other side of the yard, where two little girls were running around. Sienna was stomping around after the girls, her face twisted in what Fox assumed was a monster's grimace.

Fox couldn't help but smile a little at her silliness. There were two cameras roving around, but they were focused on the BBQ pit and Audrey, who was currently talking with her mom.

Was Sienna actually having fun with these girls because she wanted to? Fox doubted it. His guess was that she was hoping her little show would catch the attention of the camera crew, and she'd be able to showcase her "human" side.

The two girls ran to their dad, with Sienna close behind. She was still making the monster face, and now Fox could hear the sound effects that went along with it.

He chuckled a little, and the sound drew Sienna's attention.

She stopped next to Fox, hands on her hips. "Are you laughing at my terrifying toothless tarantula monster?"

He bit his lip, but a smile still tugged at his lips. "I wouldn't dare."

"I'll have you know it's terrifying."

She looked so serious that Fox let out another involuntary chuckle.

"She *is* scary," said the littlest girl. She turned to Oliver. "Daddy tell the scary monster to go away."

Oliver looked up from his conversation with Alex, confused, then caught Sienna's eye and smiled. "Don't worry sweetie, it's almost time for us to go. I was just telling Uncle Alex that it's time to start setting up for tonight's competition. You can come help, if you want."

The little girl jumped up and down with excitement. "Yay! I love getting to do grownup work with you."

Oliver laughed. "I doubt what we're about to do counts as 'grownup work,' but I'd love to have you tag along." He led his daughters away, and Alex followed.

Since Eli had wandered off at some point to stand by Audrey, that left Fox and Sienna alone.

Seeing everything Oliver and Alex had built gave Fox a strange unsettled feeling. They were the same age as he was, yet he'd barely done anything worthwhile so far in his life. And here Eli was, with a job he loved, about to start his family. It stirred something unfamiliar and a little scary in Fox.

"You must be relieved," Fox said to Sienna, in an effort to get his mind off of whatever random emotions the higher altitude must be giving him.

Sienna raised an eyebrow. "Relieved?"

"You don't have to put on that show for the girls and the cameras anymore."

"Of course it was a show, I'm an actor." A crease formed between her brows. "But believe it or not, I was doing that to make them laugh, not for the cameras."

Now Fox raised an eyebrow. "Well, I guess that's probably true. You did look pretty ridiculous. It was a nice change from that perfect mask you wear all the time."

"It's not a mask, and I'm not trying to be perfect. I just want to be my best."

"Not your best is okay sometimes, you know."

She crossed her arms over her chest. "No, it's not."

"I'm far from perfect most of the time," he said. "But I like to think I'm okay."

She bit her lip and looked up at him through lowered lids. A shoulder lifted in a shrug. "You're not terrible."

He cleared his throat, ignoring the strange pull in his chest. "If you're buttering me up just to get me to play some of Audrey's music at the wedding, it's not happening."

Sienna uncrossed her arms and put them back on her hips. "You just had to rub it in, didn't you? You beat us by thirty seconds. I demand a recount."

Fox grinned. The thrill of winning against Sienna overpowered whatever weird feelings he'd just had. It must have been the spicy BBQ sauce getting to his stomach. Definitely not her. "Look, I'm not even scowling, I'm so happy."

"Happy because you get to play stuff like Bryan Adams and Savage Garden instead of that new-fangled noise the youth of today call music?"

Fox choked. Those bands were popular when he was younger, but he couldn't remember the last time he'd listened to something by either of them. "How old do you think I am?"

She tapped a finger on her chin and considered him carefully. "Hmm...somewhere between roaming the earth with the dinosaurs and knowing Julius Caesar personally." Her eyes were narrowed, but the curve of her mouth was playful.

Not that Fox noticed her mouth—or the way it curved. "I'm the same age as Audrey and Eli, you know."

"And yet, you seem decades older."

Fox didn't get a chance to counter before he felt a hand on his shoulder. His smile fell when he saw it was Bruce.

"How are my team leads doing?" Bruce asked, a cameraman positioned right behind him. "You're tied heading into tonight's competition."

"This afternoon was a fluke," said Sienna, her playfulness gone in the blink of an eye. Her eyebrows drew together, and her eyes had turned icy. It was like the grownup version of the terrifying monster she'd used on the girls, and Fox knew she was back to playing her role for the cameras. "We're winning everything else."

Bruce laughed, loud and right in Fox's ear, making Fox grimace. Which, he realized, was probably exactly what Bruce wanted to get on camera.

"But the music, that was important to Audrey, wasn't it?" Bruce said. "Must be tough, putting something that big into the hands of the groomsmen."

Fox bristled at this. As much as he didn't want to rise to Bruce's bait, he had to defend himself. "I think we'll do a much better job than the bridesmaids with the music."

"And you're the expert?" Sienna cocked an eyebrow and perfectly tilted her head to catch the afternoon light.

"Yes," Fox answered, then kept his mouth closed, not wanting to give Bruce anymore details—or ammunition—than that. He and the other groomsmen would put together an amazing soundtrack for the reception, and no one needed to know the reasons he truly was the expert here.

"Oh ho!" Bruce patted Fox's back. "Sounds like the tension's really heating up. That should make tonight even more interesting. What's your strategy for dealing with the unexpected?"

Sienna jumped in, saying something about getting into their opponent's head and keeping their eyes on the prize. A bunch of generic soundbites that would make for good television.

Meanwhile, Fox was eagerly waiting for Bruce—and the cameras—to leave.

*Just eight more days,* he told himself as Bruce continued chatting with Sienna, her face bright from the attention. If he could hang in just another week, there'd be no more fake reactions, no more cameras, and no more Sienna.

Fox was only partially sure that the tightness in his chest was from the brisket, and not from the thought of life without the terrifying toothless tarantula monster.

8 Days Until Dream Wedding

SIENNA PUT on a tough face for the camera, but she was serious. The girls were winning everything else.

Losing control of the music hadn't been that disastrous. Even Sienna had to admit her older sister had some, ah, *questionable* favorites. But that didn't stop Audrey from shaking her booty on the dancefloor at every possible opportunity, which was always entertaining. And not because Audrey was a good dancer.

Unfortunately, all the performer genes had gone to Sienna, which before today, she'd been happy about. Now it would serve them all better if Audrey and Harper were at least a tiny bit coordinated, and better at playing things up for the camera.

Maybe then she could turn off her onscreen persona for more than a couple of minutes at a time. Maybe Fox would get off her back about it.

Thankfully, that evening's contest was making s'mores. This was Harper's arena, and it would mean Sienna would get her much-desired reprieve.

"Can we do anything else to help you?" Reagan

asked, her hands full of sticks. Audrey was taking them one by one and squishing marshmallows to the ends before lining them up along the rocks surrounding the campfire.

The girls were at the edge of the property, with the trees and mountains in the background. It would look amazing on camera, and Sienna had to wonder if the local tourism board knew how much free publicity Wellspring would be getting once this aired.

If *this airs*, thought Sienna.

Would Bruce pull the plug if Harry did end up leaving early? He was still here, for now, poking at one of the guys' fires with one hand, the other typing furiously on his phone.

Harper shook her head. "Just keep those marshmallows coming. Remember, do *not* burn them."

Audrey stuck out her lower lip. "But they taste so much better that way."

"Not everyone likes their dessert to taste like charcoal," Harper argued.

"And not everyone likes things sickeningly sweet."

The two sisters started bickering around the familiar topic that had started causing problems since their Girl Scout days.

Sienna giggled. It felt like a typical summer night from when they were all kids. She went over to Audrey and wrapped her arms around her shoulders. "I missed this. I've missed you guys."

Audrey smiled. "Well, we've been here. You're the one with the big fancy acting career in New York."

Sienna laughed her brightest laugh, but her stomach dropped.

If only they knew how very close she was to

having to come back home for good, tail between her legs, a failure in every possible way. Her phone lay heavy in her pocket, dozens of unread messages she didn't have to read to know what they said. Her landlord couldn't really fulfill his threats in just two days, could he?

Sienna watched as Harper assembled all the ingredients into the most perfect s'mores. You wouldn't think something like this campfire staple could be so complex, and yet, Harper made it look almost gourmet with her unique spin and presentation.

Of course, that left the rest of the girls with very little to do.

Even if the music was in good hands, Sienna felt the sting of losing the last competition, and now faced with the inability to do much to help win the current one, she made her way over to the boys' side.

There had been no instructions against talking to each other during the competition, just no touching each other's ingredients or fires. Talking to Fox would not only give her something to do, but it might make for some good television too. Harper's assembly line was mesmerizing, there was only so much screen time it could fill.

Bruce's eyes tracked Sienna as she wandered over to where Fox was sitting. It was clear he was judging if it would be worth it to pull a camera off of the cooks to capture whatever would happen between the two of them.

*Put your camera on us*, she thought as she got closer to Eli and the groomsmen. Sienna hated that she needed to play into Bruce's expectations to get the air time and attention she needed, but what other choice did she have? And the best way to do that was to create more tension with Fox.

Sienna approached Fox from behind, so he wouldn't notice her. He was on his own at the smallest of the three fires, holding a marshmallow close to the middle of the flame while looking out into the trees. He was humming softly to himself and looked so peaceful, she almost hated to interrupt.

"I don't know why you guys are even trying," she said, snickering when he jumped a bit at the sound of her voice. "You do know Harper is the best baker in three counties, right?"

Fox opened his mouth, but then snapped it shut when the cameraman started to set up across from them.

Why did he always clam up like this? She'd seen him smile with the guys. She'd enjoyed their banter about music this afternoon before Bruce had shown up. If only Fox would actually talk to her when the cameras were rolling, it was sure to get Bruce's attention in the editing room.

She took a seat next to Fox on the log and watched as he held his marshmallow above the flames. He lowered the stick into the flames and held it there. If he wasn't careful, it was going to catch on fire.

"You're burning your marshmallow," Sienna said, reaching for his stick.

He jerked it away. "You're not supposed to touch our stuff."

Sienna felt her cheeks warm, and not from her proximity to the fire. She wasn't thinking about the rules, only that his marshmallow was about to turn black. "I just didn't think you'd want to ruin it."

"Audrey isn't the only one who likes them burned."

"Wait." Sienna blinked. "How do you know that Audrey likes her marshmallows that way?"

Fox shrugged. "I've known Eli and Audrey for over a decade. Ever since you were in diapers probably."

"Ha ha, very funny. I was in middle school ten years ago, thank you very much."

"And I was in college." He leaned in and whispered. "You were still a *kid*."

"Well, I'm not a kid anymore." She pushed back her shoulders. "Besides, I've always been mature for my age."

"You, mature?" He laughed. "I'd like to see that."

Sienna crossed her arms and stuck out her tongue.

Fox laughed. "Did you seriously just stick your tongue out at me? On camera?"

She gasped, her head turning to where the blinking red light reminded her everything she was doing was caught on film. Somehow in the midst of their back and forth, she'd managed to forget that. And she *never* forgot about the cameras.

What was this guy doing to her?

"Well, you're a jerk," she managed to say as she attempted to school her features.

"Good one."

Silence descended between them. She looked over at him and was struck by the quiet beauty of the scene before her: his sharp jawline lit by the firelight, the trees swaying in the background, and the blue sky streaked with violet as the sun began to set. If Bruce had any sense, he'd make this the opening shot to every episode, and the viewers would be glued to their screens.

The crackling of the fire was barely audible over the sounds of Wade and Eli fighting about chocolate placement and Harper's never-ending lecture on the ingredients she used for the homemade graham crackers that were available at her bakery.

Sienna cleared her throat. "Are you a musician?"

Fox gave her a sharp look. "Why would you ask that?"

"Just trying to make conversation."

He continued to stare.

"Earlier, when Bruce asked if you were an expert on music, you said yes without hesitation. Plus, you were so happy to win the music challenge." Sienna shrugged. "Then, when I walked up, you were humming, so I just thought maybe you were a musician or something."

Fox glanced at the camera before jerking his head ever so slightly.

Sienna leaned in and the cool night breeze at her back—not the sudden proximity to Fox—made her shiver a little.

"I used to be, but I don't like to talk about it. It was a long time ago."

She smirked. "Back when I was in diapers?"

The corner of his mouth ticked up. "Before that even."

Sienna's heart skipped a beat, and she knew it had to be from a lack of food. Lunch had been hours ago. She dropped her hand into the bag of marshmallows at Fox's feet and popped one into her mouth. A growling stomach on camera was not appropriate. "So, what's the great music you're going to play at the wedding?"

Fox leaned back a bit, and Sienna breathed a sigh that was a weird mix of relief and disappointment before she reached for another marshmallow.

"Stop touching our stuff," Fox said with a scowl and

snatched the bag up.

Sienna relaxed. The cantankerous Fox she knew was back, and she could handle him much better than the Fox who had just smiled at her. "Harper won't let me touch anything. I'm kind of a disaster in the kitchen."

His eyes went wide. "You're actually admitting you're bad at something?"

Sienna waved a hand. "Lots of people aren't good cooks. Especially in New York where you can't go three feet without hitting a Michelin-Starred restaurant."

"And those are the kinds of places you're used to eating at?"

Sienna shifted on the log. There was no way she was going to admit she'd been living on Ramen and peanut butter and jelly sandwiches for the last month. She wasn't going to admit to anyone—on camera or off—all the dirty details of her life as a struggling actor. Especially not to Fox.

"What's with the twenty questions?"

"Just trying to make conversation," he said. And she couldn't be sure if the fire was playing tricks on her, but she swore there was a twinkle in his eye when he said it.

"Then why don't you tell me about this awesome music you have planned for the reception."

"You'll have to wait and see." Fox grinned. "Patience is something grownups are good at. Practice will do you good."

Sienna was tempted to stick her tongue out again but remembered just in time about the camera.

"I look forward to it," she said instead, a wide smile of her own plastered on her face. "It looks like Harper is nearly done with her masterpiece. I hope you enjoy the menu the girls pick out."

"As long as it's not fish, I'll be happy."

Sienna frowned at that but got up before she was tempted to say anything else.

She hoped whatever they'd gotten on camera had been enough to make Bruce happy. It had not gone the way she'd intended. Her emotions had been all over the place, she'd reacted out of instinct instead of a calm center, and the words had flown out of her mouth without even thinking.

Basically, it had been the opposite of acting. She'd been herself with him. And she wasn't sure what to think about that.

———

LATER THAT NIGHT, when the competition was over, and the cameras were off for the night, Sienna snuck over to the room Audrey and Reagan shared. She pressed her ear to the door and was surprised to hear laughter ringing out from the other side.

Good, she wasn't the only one still awake, or celebrating the bridesmaids' second win. Harper's butterscotch and apple s'mores had been incredible.

Sienna knocked softly on the door.

"Who is it?" said a singsong voice.

"Who do you think?" Sienna whispered.

The door swung open, and she was greeted by Harper's smiling face.

Reagan's head was visible next to Audrey on the bed. Was everyone hanging out together without her?

Sienna didn't have time to dwell on it, because Harper quickly looked up and down the hall before she pulled Sienna inside and shut the door behind them.

"What's going on?" she asked as she looked around the room.

"We were just having some girl time after today's events," Audrey answered. "And because the cameramen think we're asleep, we get to do it without their watchful eye."

"Without me?"

Harper wrapped her arm around Sienna's shoulders. "We didn't think you'd want to come. You looked pretty upset after the s'more competition, even though we won thanks to yours truly."

"Honestly, Sienna. You were so grumpy all day. We figured you'd want to sit this one out. Get some beauty sleep for the cameras tomorrow." Audrey stretched out on the bed and put her hands behind her head.

Is that really what they thought about her? That she only cared about how she looked?

Sure, she'd been caught up in the show, and wanting to make an effort to look good for filming, but she cared about her family more than *Wedding Games* and what it could do for her career.

Her sister was getting married, after all. That was a big deal. Bigger than any contract she might get from the exposure.

"Why *were* you so grumpy anyway?" Harper asked.

"I bet it was Fox." Reagan crossed her arms with a knowing smile.

Sienna's cheeks warmed. "Fox is the grumpy one, not me."

"Look." Harper clapped her hands with unashamed glee. "She's blushing. You know what that means."

"Do you like Fox?" Audrey asked. She sat up and bounced slightly on the bed with a sly smile on her lips.

Sienna snorted. "Uh, absolutely not."

"Oh, my goodness." Harper's eyes went wide. "You do."

Sienna struggled to keep her cool but forced a smile. She sat down on the fancy upholstered chair facing the bed. "No," she said slowly. "He said some things about me being immature, and it hurt my feelings. I do *not* like him."

She could appreciate a nice set of muscles and a gorgeous head of hair, but they couldn't go two minutes without teasing each other. Still, he had his moments...

She expected her sisters and Reagan to keep teasing her but was met with laughter. "What?"

"Nothing," Audrey said. "I just don't think I've seen anyone get under Fox's skin like you have. Or vice versa."

"And that's funny because...?"

"Because he's usually so chill about everything," Audrey said with a shrug. "He doesn't let himself get riled up."

Reagan nodded from beside her. "Or at least he hasn't since he stopped playing."

Sienna leaned forward in the chair. Between the burned marshmallows and the room party and now Fox's music, it felt like she was the last to know everything. She took a deep breath. "What happened? Why did he stop playing?"

Audrey bit her lip and looked at Reagan. "I don't know..."

"Oh, come on," Sienna said and threw up her hands. "He started to tell me about it tonight. Said it was a long time ago but didn't say any more because of the cameras."

Audrey let out a long sigh. "Fox used to play a lot."

"Like, you're hanging out and he's the guy playing something on his guitar in the background, a lot," Reagan said.

"Yeah." Audrey nodded. "And sometimes it was really annoying. But he was good, Sienna. Really good. He even got a contract with a label."

Sienna sat up straight. Fox had a contract with a record label?

"But then B—" Audrey stopped and pressed her lips together for a brief moment before she continued. "Let's just say a lot of stuff happened, and Fox walked away from it all. He stopped playing guitar and stopped singing. He moved to another state and started working on boats. He's avoided people and crowds since then."

"Honestly, it's a miracle Eli convinced him to come on *Wedding Games*," Reagan said to Audrey, who nodded again.

The room fell silent.

Sienna tried to reconcile the image of Fox rocking out on the guitar with his withdrawn and surly demeanor. "So, what was the 'stuff' that made him give up music?"

"Nope." Audrey shook her head. "That is not my story to tell. If you really want to know, you're going to have to ask him."

"Oh, I plan to," Sienna said.

He clearly still loved music. She couldn't imagine having a shot at success and then just walking away just because "a lot of stuff happened". But she didn't like the worried look on Audrey's face. What if the same kind of stuff could happen to her?

## 7 Days Until Dream Wedding

FINALLY, Fox was alone.

Yesterday had been intense. The obstacle course in the morning, then the barbecue, then the s'mores contest. People around him all the time, asking questions, telling him where to stand and where to sit. The cameras had been everywhere.

Sienna had been everywhere.

He needed a break, and the production schedule had thankfully given him just that. They were filming something with just Audrey, Eli, and both sets of parents. No need for Fox to be anywhere specific before 1 p.m.

He'd set his alarm for as early as he could manage and headed out immediately onto one of the trails that began at the edge of the property. He inhaled deeply as he stepped into the comforting shade of the trees, and it felt like the first breath he'd taken all week.

Eli had brought up the idea again last night of Wade and Fox finding jobs closer to Wellspring. Breathing in the mountain air, Fox was seriously tempted. The only problem was that he'd been working on boat motors for the past ten years, and he was pretty sure there wasn't much need for that up in the mountains of the western part of the state.

Still, he'd reinvented himself once when he'd needed to, and Eli had been a big help with that. Doing it again wouldn't be that difficult. But what would he do? What did he even like to do? When he wasn't working, he was either sleeping or finding excuses not to play. He hadn't picked up his guitar in months.

But being here in Wellspring changed everything. Seeing green everywhere he looked, and inhaling the familiar scent of wet earth, made him feel alive for the first time in years. The slight nagging desire to sing—the one he always felt humming just below the surface—intensified the further he walked into the woods until it became unbearable. He needed to sing, and just the thought of doing that in the mountains made him feel a little too much like Julie Andrews in *The Sound of Music*.

But as long as Fox could keep himself from twirling around in a circle with his arms outstretched, it might be okay.

It started low, as he hummed the melody of a song he'd written in college—before everything was ruined. And soon that hum became quiet singing. When he finished the first song, he moved onto another. When he got to the chorus, he let his voice get a little louder.

And then louder still, until his voice drowned out every other sound.

He belted out the last verse, feeling even more ridiculous than when he'd started. But man, it felt good to sing.

At least until he turned around the bend and saw Sienna standing there.

Of course she would appear when he wanted nothing more than to be alone.

She wasn't walking, instead leaning against a tree like she was in the middle of a photo shoot.

Panic shot through Fox's veins, and he looked around. No, there were no cameras. That's just the way she stood, apparently, like the whole world was looking at her.

He certainly was right now.

"You know, most people move when they're hiking," he said, stopping a few feet away from her. His heart was pounding. Maybe she hadn't heard his singing.

"You know, most people who sing like that don't just give it up for no reason."

Or maybe she'd heard it all.

"I don't sing that well. And I didn't give up for no reason. I had a *great* reason." He walked past her. "Maybe I don't like talking about it with strangers in the woods."

Though "stranger" wasn't exactly a fitting description of Sienna. In just a few days, she'd learned more about him than he'd ever shared with his colleagues he'd known for years. And soon, she'd be his best friend's sister-in-law.

Regardless, he didn't want to talk about it with *anyone*.

"Audrey told me you were amazing on the guitar," she said, following him down the trail. "That you had a record deal."

"Audrey shouldn't have told you that. That's all in the past."

She walked in front of him and stopped, hands on her hips. He pulled up short to avoid plowing into her.

"There's only two reasons someone with that much talent gives up." She held up a finger. "Either you partied too hard, and they dropped you for your antics, or you choked during a major performance, and they dropped you."

Fox snorted. If only one of the options she provided was the reason. He pushed past her, refusing to give her an answer.

Unfortunately, she followed, not picking up on the obvious I-don't-want-to-talk-about-it vibe he was throwing out with his silent retreat.

"Did you get stage fright?"

Fox rolled his eyes but kept walking.

"Crazy stalkers who carried locks of your hair in a locket around their neck?"

Like he'd even gotten close to that level of fame.

"How about—"

Fox spun on his heels and faced Sienna. "How about my girlfriend, and co-writer, ditched me the second she came across someone more famous and took all my songs with her. Let's just say, it was really hard to finish the album after that."

Sienna's mouth dropped open. For once in her life, she appeared to be speechless.

"Like I said, I don't want to talk about it." He gave her one last hard look before he turned back around and started walking down the trail again.

And yet, she still followed him.

Fox growled under his breath. Did she ever pick up on body language? It seemed like a glaring problem for someone whose very job depended on portraying different personalities.

"I can't even imagine my life without acting," she said, surprisingly close behind as Fox picked up his pace. "How have you gone ten years without performing?"

"I just have, okay? Not all of us crave the spotlight." Or the fall into destructive despair when the spotlight lures away your girlfriend.

"You're saying that if given the chance, you wouldn't be happy in front of a crowd shouting your name, begging to hear more of your music?"

He tried to picture it as he stepped over a root that was sticking out in the path. Singing his songs on stage, seeing how his words and music could touch people… Nothing was better than that. But he'd already flown too close to the sun once and gotten burned. He wasn't going to make that mistake again.

Fox turned to face her again, ignoring the vibrating quality the air seemed to take on when they were so close. "One day, you'll have that spotlight on you, and hopefully you're made of stronger stuff than I was. Hopefully you can keep your head when you're being pulled in eight-hundred different directions, and everyone wants a piece of you. I know you think it's everything you want, and I hope it's everything you want it to be when it happens. But it's just not the life for me."

Two lines appeared between her eyebrows. "Is that why you work on boats? Some sort of penance for what-ever you did when you were a kid?"

"I wasn't a kid, I was—"

"You were my age." Sienna stuck out her chin. "And believe me when I say guys my age are way more immature than the girls. So, you were basically a kid."

Fox closed his eyes again and took a deep breath. She didn't understand, she couldn't. It wasn't just what Becky did to Fox, but what Fox had done afterward. He had been so out of control—and had ruined so many lives—there was no way he could ever go back.

He didn't deserve to get another chance, no matter how much he missed it.

"Why is this so important to you?" he asked, opening his eyes to see her staring at him with a rosy cheeked perfection from the hike. "Why do you care?"

Her cheeks turned an even darker pink, and she looked at the ground. "I just think there's more to you than grumpy Grandpa Fox."

A corner of his mouth tipped up against his will.

"It's why I came out here today," she said. "It's why I stopped on the trail when I heard you singing. It's a shame you feel like you can't do something you're so good at and clearly love so much."

"I do love it," he said softly, staring off into the trees. "More than anything. But sometimes it's the things we love the most that can destroy us."

"Or make us stronger."

Somehow, during their conversation, they'd inched closer and closer to one another. And with Sienna's words hanging in the air, Fox looked at her. Really looked at her.

Her bright blue eyes stared up at him, as the rest of her face was way more relaxed than when there were other people—and cameras—around.

She was gorgeous, and when Fox realized why, he could have smacked himself.

She wasn't putting on a show anymore.

And suddenly, he wanted to tell her everything.

He hadn't even told Eli everything. His best friend had been happy just to see Fox alive and hadn't asked too many questions. But here, alone in the woods, he wanted to open up about Becky, the self-destructive path he'd gone down after she'd left him, and the hole in his chest that had opened up and never seemed to get any less painful when he stopped playing music.

"I—" He stopped at the sound of footsteps and muffled voices and turned his head.

The cameras.

The contract stated they could film anywhere that wasn't considered a "safe space." It didn't matter if he was in the inn or the woods, alone or with Sienna, they could pop in at any time. And somehow, they'd noticed the two of them were up here.

He quickly stepped back from Sienna, hoping to put some distance between the two of them before the cameras captured anything.

*Was it too late?*

He looked back at her and the real, caring girl was gone, hidden behind a perfect facade that the world would see as beautiful, but Fox only saw as fake. Everything from her posture to her expression was manufactured with the audience in mind.

When Jason Castle came walking up behind them, Fox wanted to find the nearest hole and bury himself inside.

But Sienna had her game face on.

"What do we have here?" Jason said as he got closer. "A secret battle between team leaders? Or is this a case of flirting with the enemy?"

Sienna laughed as she gave Jason's shoulder a friendly shove. "I can promise you there's none of that going on here. Nothing's going to get in my way of winning the rest of the competitions for my sister."

She turned to face Fox, and gave him a small, almost imperceivable nod.

"Yeah," he said, his voice flat.

Sienna narrowed her eyes a tiny bit at him.

Jason stared at him for a moment longer, waiting for Fox to continue. But he didn't know what else to say. He hated the cameras, he didn't care about the competitions, and he couldn't care less about putting on a facade for everyone.

When Jason realized he wouldn't be getting anymore material from Fox, he turned back to Sienna. She started going on about the s'more victory and her strategy for the next game.

Watching her performance made Fox feel sick to his stomach. He walked over to the edge of the path and looked out over the mountains.

Five minutes ago, Sienna had been the most beautiful girl in the world.

Five minutes ago, he'd felt brave for the first time in over a decade.

A lot could change in five minutes.

## 7 Days Until Dream Wedding

---

Sienna was relieved when Jason finally finished grilling her.

Of course, she wanted to make sure she did everything in her power to get noticed, but as much as she loved being in front of the camera, it was the last place she wanted to be this morning. She had gotten so close to a breakthrough with Fox.

It had taken a lot of effort to ask questions while trying to keep pace with Fox as he hiked through the mountains, but she'd done it. And Sienna knew he had been just about to open up to her.

She'd gotten a tiny little peek at that kind and loyal side of him she kept hearing so much about. The hints she'd seen over the past few days at the complex, yet caring man were finally giving way to the deeper layers underneath.

But the real question was, why did she care so much?

"It's been lovely chatting with you, Sienna," Jason said with a smile. He looked down at his phone. "But apparently, Wade is trying to convince Eli to get a tattoo in honor of his upcoming wedding."

"And Eli is actually considering it?" Sienna didn't have to try very hard to put on her most surprised and concerned face for the camera.

"Sounds like it. Bruce wants us all down there STAT. Catch up quick, okay? I think you'd do great in the middle of this drama."

Sienna nodded then waved goodbye to Jason and the cameramen as they started walking down the path back to the Emerald Inn.

When she turned to look for Fox, she expected him to be far ahead down the path, but he was still standing off to the side, looking over the mountains in the distance.

She walked over to him. "Hey."

He grunted in response.

"Jason said we need to head back down just in case things escalate down there."

"I heard. I didn't realize tattoos were such a big deal."

Really? And here Sienna thought Fox knew everything about Audrey. She loved having information Fox didn't. "They are to Audrey."

There was a moment of hesitation, as if Fox was trying to decide if he wanted to ask or not. But she could see in his eyes the instant his curiosity became too much to bear. "What do you mean?"

Sienna stopped her lips from forming into a huge, I-know-more-than-you grin. "Maybe you've noticed Audrey doesn't have any tattoos."

Fox shrugged. "I guess. I've honestly never noticed. They're not a big deal."

"For most people they aren't, but I can tell you for a fact Audrey has an unreasonable vendetta against them. And no, I don't get it either."

"What about Wade? He's covered in them, and she seems to like him just fine."

"Obviously she adores Wade." Sienna rolled her eyes. "But she's not marrying him. She would flip her lid if Eli got one."

Rather than the grumpy sigh she was expecting, Fox's eyebrows shot up, and he turned away from the view with sudden purpose. "Well, then we'd better get down there and make sure nothing happens to mess up this wedding."

Sienna smiled. "Sounds like a plan."

She couldn't believe it. *This* was the attitude a best man should have. Playing nice for the cameras was all well and good, but this was how to show he really did care about Audrey and Eli's happily ever after. The more time she spent with Fox, the more she saw he wasn't as horrible as she thought that first day.

The two started walking back toward the Emerald Inn. The path was uneven and rocky, so the two moved slowly. Any closeness they may or may not have been on the brink of sharing before Jason showed up was gone, and the silence between them was unbearable.

Sienna waited for Fox to say something, but his attention was on the ground at their feet. It was a twenty-minute hike back down—a long, agonizing twenty minutes if Fox continued his silent treatment.

Sienna picked up the pace. There was no way she could handle much more of this, and she wasn't going to be the one to break the silence. She concentrated on stepping over small branches that littered the path and was doing just fine until her toe caught a rock that was sticking up out of the ground.

She tipped forward, and her arms swung out around her. Thankfully, dance training kept her from crashing into the ground, but she did come down on one knee pretty hard. Embarrassed, she bit her cheek to keep from crying out.

Sienna was surprised when Fox didn't make a snide comment about being more careful, but not nearly as surprised as when she felt Fox at her side, and he extended his hand. It brushed against hers and lingered there for a few moments before she finally took it. Without a word, he pulled her up. And then he kept her hand in his.

Sienna tried to steady her breathing and her racing heart without much success.

When she looked up at him in question, he only shrugged in response. His face was the same serious expression he usually wore, but at least there was no scowl. He was obviously just helping her keep her balance, but Sienna liked the way her hand felt in his and barely resisted the urge to rub her thumb over the back of it.

As they continued down the path, Fox would occasionally tighten his grip to help her balance better. Sienna wanted to tell him that she didn't need his help, but she also didn't want to risk a fall. At least that's what she told herself when she squeezed back whenever she walked over a particularly rocky area.

They continued like this for several minutes before Fox cleared his throat. "I like you better when the cameras aren't around."

The words would have felt insulting if it wasn't for

Fox's gentle tone—or the fact that he was still holding her hand.

Sienna looked back up at him. "What do you mean?"

"You just turn into this different person when they're pointed at you, like you're trying so hard to make them like you."

*And that was a bad thing?*

She took a deep breath. "My career depends on the camera liking me. Could you imagine watching a show where the main character was grumpy all the time?"

Fox snorted. "We're back to this again?"

She bit her lip. "I actually don't think you're Mr. Grumpy anymore," she said softly.

Fox lifted a brow and waited for her to continue.

Sienna's heart raced for a completely different reason. Fox had been really open with her up on the mountain. He'd told her about his ex-girlfriend, who sounded like a horrible person, and how he missed music so much it left a hole in his chest. She could trust him with a little bit of her pain, couldn't she?

"I think I understand you a little more now," she said.

His mouth turned down. "From one embarrassing conversation?"

She laughed. "It's not that embarrassing."

He shook his head. "Maybe not for you."

"Seriously, I think I get it." She took a deep breath. "I've always wanted to be an actor. Since I was a little girl."

"I think every little girl wants to be an actress or a ballerina," Fox said. "I wanted to be an astronaut."

"But most kids outgrow those dreams, right?"

He nodded slowly. "Right."

"Well, I didn't. The older I got the more I realized it was the only thing I wanted out of life. I joined drama club freshman year and put my entire self into it. I was getting lead roles my sophomore year and was the president of the club my junior and senior year."

Fox tipped his head. "Impressive."

"Thanks," Sienna mumbled and looked down briefly before continuing. The path was leveling out, but her hand was still firmly clasped in his. "My mother was so proud of me until I told her my plan to pursue acting as a career. She thought it was something I was doing for fun in high school, but when she realized that I wanted a life on the stage and in front of the camera, well, let's just say she wasn't too happy about it."

"But it sounds like you've followed through. Eli said you live near the city and have been on TV and Broadway."

"Yeah…"

Sienna had been cast for a few roles here and there, but none of them were the big break she so desperately needed. And ageism was alive and well in the entertainment business. She was only a few years away from becoming an old maid in the eyes of casting directors, and with every passing day, she felt time running out to make it big.

"So, what does it matter if your mom doesn't approve? She's got to love you regardless. It's part of the mom gig. Mine still did, no matter what dumb stuff I did as a kid."

Sienna frowned and looked down. Of course her mother still loved her. But she wasn't proud of Sienna, not the way she was of Harper for starting her own business, or of Audrey for the teaching awards she won. Her mother's love couldn't buy Sienna groceries, or pay her rent, or even write a strongly worded letter to her landlord insisting he didn't kick Sienna and her roommate out for being late on said rent.

Not that she could say any of that to Fox.

"Have you ever considered that maybe your mom misses you?" Fox asked.

Sienna looked up.

"It's possible she wants you closer to her." He shrugged. "Being far from family and friends is hard sometimes, even if it's to do something we love."

Luckily, Sienna wouldn't have to explore that line of thought too deeply. They were back at the Emerald Inn. Those long twenty minutes had felt like five.

"There you are," Bruce called out as he walked across the grassy lawn. "Austin showed me some of the footage they got of you two on the hike. Really great stuff, guys."

Sienna's heart skipped a beat. Bruce liked what he saw? That was great news.

"We'd really like to get some more of you two together. I think we can really play up this relationship that's growing between the head of both teams, what do you think?"

Sienna felt her face heat. The word *relationship* made it sound like something much more romantic—which it wasn't. This was just a case of Sienna trying to be friends with Fox for her sister's sake. But maybe it could show some of Sienna's range.

"I think it's a great idea," she answered before she turned to face Fox, who had pulled his hand away from Sienna's the moment Bruce had shown up.

Fox's lips were pressed together in a hard line, his posture stiff. Sienna's heart sank.

"Come on, this will be great for the show. It'll be good for Eli and Audrey," Sienna said. She widened her eyes into her patented puppy-dog stare that had gotten her older sisters to do almost anything for her as a kid.

"Sure." Fox sighed. "Anything for Audrey and Eli."

Then he turned on his heel and walked away toward the inn. Sienna couldn't understand why he was so upset. She knew he wasn't an actor, but his time in the music industry must have taught him something about putting on a show. Sure, it was reality TV, not Broadway, but they still needed to be entertaining.

As she watched his dark head disappear into the inn, she fought the urge to run after him and make sure he was okay. She wanted to explain that their conversation on the hike was real, and that she really enjoyed it. Her foot took an involuntary step toward the inn, when she felt Bruce's hand on her shoulder.

"Seriously, Sienna. You really shine on screen. I see a lot of potential for you and have some friends who'd be looking for someone just like you for their next project."

Her heart nearly stopped and smiled eagerly at Bruce. "Really?"

The producer gave her a wide grin. "Absolutely. We just need to try to get Fox to be more willing to let us film him. He keeps trying to evade us, and it's not great if we can't get the best man on camera. Surely, you can see how that could have unintended consequences for the show. He might not get it, but I know you have experience in the movie business."

*Unintended consequences?* Her chest tightened, and she tried to think of which of the thousand clauses she'd be in danger of breaking if she said no. Would they pull the plug before Audrey and Eli got their wedding?

Bruce gave her shoulder a gentle squeeze. "Can I count on you to help me out with that?"

Sienna straightened her shoulders and gave him the best smile she could muster with the dread pooling in her stomach. "Absolutely."

## THIRTEEN

7 Days Until Dream Wedding

---

"I STILL CAN'T BELIEVE you wussed out with the tattoo," Wade said as the guys all made their way down to the dining room. He rolled up his shirt to show off the sleeve that covered most of his arm—and the new addition he'd had done earlier that day. It was still covered with a bandage, but everyone knew he'd gotten a clapperboard to commemorate his time on TV. "It doesn't hurt."

Eli poked the newly inked space on Wade's arm, causing his freshly tattooed friend to grimace. "I'm not afraid of it hurting."

"Then why didn't you get one with me?" he asked, pulling his shirt back down.

"I—"

"Because he's whipped," Harry interrupted as he trailed behind the guys.

Fox didn't think Harry had even been paying attention to the conversation, too busy typing away on the screen of his phone. But apparently Harry had an uncanny ability to multitask.

Fox turned to Eli, whose face was turning a deep shade of red. It wasn't the first time someone had accused his best friend of bending over backward for Audrey, but Fox knew it upset Eli every single time. Fox was just thankful there were no cameras here right now since they were all set up in the dining hall for tonight's competition.

But really, whose business was it if Eli was a romantic and wanted to make Audrey happy? It was more than could be said for Harry, who always looked like it was a major inconvenience for him to do anything but stare at his phone and make rude remarks to Reagan.

Did Harry think the other guys didn't hear the way he spoke down to her? Or see the way her face fell every time he did so?

Fox took a deep breath and, as he let it out, realized no one had said anything in response to Harry's nasty comment yet. "So, what do you think tonight's competition is going to be?" he asked in an effort to break the tension he could feel building in the air.

"Does it matter?" came Harry's snide response.

*Seriously?*

Fox pinched the bridge of his nose. Could Harry not see what Fox was trying to do here? Or did he just not care?

Fox stopped and faced Harry. With a tight-lipped smile, he said, "We'd be happy to let you sit this one out."

Harry put his phone in his pocket. "What's that supposed to mean?"

"It means you're the only person who doesn't seem

to give a crap about the wedding. You haven't put that phone away the entire time."

"It's my job."

"And you're so important, you can't take a five-minute break from it?" Fox said.

"You know what? I'm not going to sit here and take this from some washed up has-been." Harry pushed past the other guys. "I'll see you down there."

*Washed up has-been?*

Fox opened his mouth to tell Harry where he could shove that stupid phone of his, but Eli stepped in front of him and put a hand on his chest.

"Listen, Fox. I don't like the guy either, okay?" He turned and looked in the direction Harry had just stormed off in before facing Fox once more. "But in about ten minutes, all the cameras are going to be pointed on us, and I don't want to mess anything up."

Fox almost laughed. Fighting was exactly what Bruce wanted to see on camera. It would give him the drama he was so badly trying to manufacture. "But—"

"But we're going to go downstairs with bright smiles on our faces," Eli said. "We're going to act like we like Harry and that we give a crap about this competition. Do you want to know why?"

"Because that's what Audrey would want?"

Eli chuckled. "Yeah, that's part of it. But it's also because if we make a big deal out of this and start ostracizing Harry, it's going to look really bad on the show. We're going to look like the bad guys."

Now Eli was concerned about how he'd look to the audience? Apparently, Sienna's desire to save face whenever the cameras were around was becoming contagious.

Fox didn't like that one bit. It was one thing for an actress to care about all of those things, but Eli was one of the best people Fox knew. He didn't want to see his friend become a two-faced phoney, no matter the reason.

"He's got a point, you know," Wade said.

Fox all but growled when he felt his friend's hand on his shoulder. He was officially ready for this week to be over. Everything about this reality show reminded him just how fake people could be, and it was overwhelming. As much as he hated his job, he would have much preferred the isolation it gave him to this.

He looked both of his friends dead in the eye to argue, to tell them they shouldn't care about what the people watching thought. But when he saw their pleading looks, he softened—just a little.

Fox sighed. *The things I do for my friends.* "Fine. I'll play nice."

———

EVERYONE FILED into the room and were directed to form a semi-circle around Jason Castle, who looked way too pleased to have so many eyes on him. "Tonight's competition is a little different from what we've done thus far," Jason announced. "Up until this point, you've been working in teams to determine one part of the upcoming wedding. Not tonight. This one's just for Eli and Audrey."

What a relief, Fox thought to himself. That meant he might have less time in front of the camera for one evening. Any respite would be something to be thankful for.

But just what did they have in store for his friends?

"Tonight is a classic newlywed game to see who knows the other better," Jason said.

Fox's nerves slipped away even more. If all he had to do was clap in the crowd while the cameras focused on the two of them, he could handle that. Especially if Harry stayed on the other side of the room.

"But that's not where it ends." Jason's smile widened and Fox's stomach sank. "There's still a role for the teams to play. How well Eli and Audrey do on the quiz will determine what materials their teams have to decorate their tables. Then those tables will be judged by the local florist and the staff of the inn, who have seen their fair share of weddings. The winning group gets to pick the bridesmaids' dresses."

From the other side of the room, Fox could see the girls' faces pale before they bent their heads together to start whispering. Of course, it had to be the dresses. What should have been a fun exchange between the future married couple was now a cutthroat competition the girls had no intention of losing.

It started off easy enough, with questions about things like favorite food and movies. Audrey and Eli were seated back to back in the middle of the room, and each held two signs labeled "bride" and "groom." When Jason asked a question, they had to hold up whichever person it was true for.

"Who was afraid of dogs as a kid?" asked Jason.

Audrey and Eli both held up the "bride" sign.

"Who takes longer to get ready in the morning?"

They both held up the "groom" sign and everyone laughed.

It was hokey, but fun. Plus, Fox didn't have to talk or do anything in particular, which suited him perfectly. He clapped when he was supposed to and laughed at Wade's antics. He scowled when Audrey got an answer right and called out suggestions to Eli to help him out. The score stayed tied through most of it.

Just when Fox was actually enjoying himself, he got the reminder that there was still more to come this evening.

"Remember, this is just part one," Jason said. "It's not whoever wins this round who gets to pick the dresses. Your score here will determine what materials you get to use for the judged challenge of table decorating."

The camera panned slowly over the two teams. Fox knew they wanted a good reaction shot but didn't have it in him to do anything more exciting than nod.

"Next question: who likes to eat their marshmallows burned?"

Audrey held up the "bride" sign, but Eli held up the "groom" sign.

Fox frowned. If he knew that about Audrey, Eli certainly did, too.

"Who wanted to play for the 49ers as a kid?"

Eli held up the "bride" sign, while Audrey waved "groom" high above her head much to everyone's amusement. But Fox wasn't laughing, he was confused. Why was Eli suddenly pretending like he didn't know anything about his fiancée—or even himself?

The reason became clear during the second break in the game to bring out the decorating supplies. Fox knew next to nothing about what a wedding table should look like, but he could see that there was some really nice stuff, and some really crappy stuff.

Eli wanted to be sure Audrey got the good stuff. Of

course he'd do that for her. What did Eli care about the bridesmaid dresses? For that matter, what did Fox care about them?

But he did care about beating Sienna. Seeing her gloating face with each wrong answer Eli gave was almost too much for Fox. Yet at the same time, her wide smile of happiness when Jason announced the girls the winners of the quiz made Fox's chest tighten in the same way it had when he'd taken her hand out in the woods.

Was it even a real smile?

Wade's disappointed face was for sure an exaggeration, and Eli had just spent half an hour feigning ignorance about the one person he knew best in the world. This whole thing was such a farce, it was all Fox could do to keep from walking out the door.

Then Sienna caught his eye and real happiness flickered across her face. His breath caught in his throat.

She was annoying and immature and obsessed with fame, but she'd gotten under his skin in a way no one ever had before.

Fox held back a groan. *Only seven more days*, he told himself as the guys made their way to a table heaped with supplies.

"Where do we even start with this?" Wade picked up a green tablecloth and held it away from his body with two fingers like it was full of spiders.

Harry let out a long sigh. "Does it even matter? Eli made sure the girls would win, why even bother?"

Fox's fist clenched at his side. He was just as annoyed about how pointless this all was, but he was here to help, even if it meant doing dumb stuff.

"Let's start by seeing what we have," said Eli, ever the optimist.

They sorted through the pile of decorations, all of which looked like it had been bought at least a decade ago. They had fresh flowers, which were pretty nice, but none of them had any clue what to do with them. The girls seemed much happier with their selection, and the sound of their giggling floated over to the guys' side of the room.

Fox kept glancing over at them, then back to his watch. How long could this go on?

"This must be pretty frustrating," Jason appeared next to the camera, looking way too happy at their confusion over the decorations. "The girls are set up nicely to win."

"Yeah thanks to Eli," said Harry, practically pouting. "Can't believe we're losing to the chicks."

"Dude, shut up," said Fox, before he could think better of it.

He was so tired of Harry's moaning and complaining. The guy wanted to win, but not to help Eli and Audrey. He just hated losing. And while Fox was pretty sure Eli's enthusiasm and Wade's goofiness were being played up for the cameras, Harry was a jerk, whether the cameras were around or not.

"Alright, alright, sounds like some tension on the team. That won't help things," Jason said. He waved a hand at another camera so there were now two focused on the guys.

"Of course there's tension, we want to win," said Wade, with a wink at the approaching camera.

"Sounds like it's mostly coming from Harry," said Jason. "Or maybe directed toward him?"

The four of them went stony silent, and Fox fought to keep his breathing even. They were always being watched so it shouldn't come as a surprise that the *Wedding Games* crew had picked up on the fact Eli, Wade, and Fox weren't too happy with the fourth member of their team.

But Fox was exceptionally annoyed tonight and wasn't about to admit that on camera.

"He's been a great addition to our group," said Eli, breaking the silence and putting an arm around Harry's shoulder. "Plus, if Reagan likes him, we like him."

Harry laughed, a tinny fake sound that grated on Fox's last nerve. "Well, Reagan thinks sliced bread is great, so the bar's set pretty low."

Jason chuckled, but none of the other guys did. Fox was getting seriously worried he'd do something stupid if he stuck around much longer. But he couldn't let the slight on Reagan stand.

"You should be thanking your lucky stars she sticks by you," said Fox. He narrowed his eyes at Harry, who glared back.

Jason whirled to face him. "Is that jealousy I hear? You've been friends with Audrey and Reagan since college, right? So maybe you're a little put out that Harry bagged her first?"

"She's not something to be won," Fox said through gritted teeth. "She's a person with feelings."

"And what do you know about her feelings?" Harry was suddenly right in front of Fox, pushing his chest into him.

"I know you treat her like she doesn't have any. It's wrong."

Harry shoved a finger into Fox's chest. "It's none of your business how I treat her."

The edges of Fox's vision were going red, and his

hands had somehow balled into fists during this short exchange. He knew it was all for the show, that Jason and Bruce were finding drama wherever they could. The worst part was, Harry totally deserved to be punched in the face, and Fox would *love* to be the one to do it.

But that's not who he was anymore. He wouldn't let some stupid reality show take away all the progress he'd made in the past ten years. He wasn't a dumb kid who used his fist to show whatever he was feeling.

So, he walked out. Without a word to anyone. He just turned away from Harry's angry face and went straight through the door into the hallway.

## 7 Days Until Dream Wedding

SIENNA DIDN'T EVEN HESITATE for a second before following Fox out of the meeting room. She ignored the startled calls of her sisters and Reagan as she made her way through the door and down the hall.

She did turn, however, when she heard Bruce's voice. Panic gripped her heart. Had she just done something that would mess things up for Audrey?

"Sienna, you were doing great in there," said Bruce, a wide smile on his face and a cameraman at his side. "The camera loves you. I can't wait for the whole team back in California to see this. You've got star written all over you."

Sienna's breath caught in her throat. The words were what she'd been waiting to hear.

"But it loves you and Fox together even more." Bruce put his hands on her shoulders. "Go find him. Get him somewhere and have him open up. This thing between you guys is television gold."

*This thing between you guys?*

Sienna's heart gave an involuntary flutter at the

thought. There was no "thing" between them. They were thrown together for this crazy show, and they'd go back to near strangers when it was over. She'd have her contacts and exposure and something decent to show casting agents, and he'd go back to his boat motors.

So why did Sienna's stomach churn at the thought of never seeing Fox again?

She plastered on a smile for Bruce. "You can count on me."

She started walking, the cameraman trailing behind her. Sienna didn't know where Fox had gone, but her first instinct told her he'd want to be somewhere away from the cameras. She hadn't been into the safe room yet but went that way now. It was a small storage room tucked beside the kitchen.

She knew Fox was behind that door. And as much as she wanted to keep Bruce happy, that wasn't why Sienna agreed to talk to him. He'd seemed really upset and she wanted to be sure he was okay. But how could she do that with a camera following her? She tried to think of a way to lose her tail, but still wanted to make Bruce happy too.

She could do both. She just needed a few minutes off screen with Fox first.

Sienna stopped and took a deep breath before she turned and smiled at the cameraman. "Give me a few minutes to talk to Fox."

The guy who was holding the camera furrowed his eyebrows.

"Look, I promise to give you some good footage, but he isn't going to leave the safe room if you're hanging right outside the door. Give me a couple of minutes, and I'll come find you, okay?"

The cameraman nodded slowly before walking down the hall.

Whew. That was easy.

Now that he was gone, she could make sure Fox was okay. Without the cameras around, she could just be herself. The thought of really opening up to Fox scared her, but also felt right. He'd told her so much in the woods. There was trust building between them.

Sienna looked down the hall to make sure the coast was clear and pushed open the door. Inside, there was a single folding chair in the midst of all the shelves of extra tablecloths and silverware. And Fox.

"Not exactly the most comfortable room to escape to, huh?" she said, closing the door behind her.

Fox looked up from where he was leaning against a shelf, his head resting on his folded arms. "I just needed a few minutes."

"I get it," she said, truly understanding the desire for solitude right now.

He raised his brows at her.

"Even the most camera-loving actors need a break every once in a while."

A corner of his mouth lifted. "Somehow I doubt that."

"Well, it's true."

Fox nodded, and the two of them stood there in silence for several moments. While they weren't touching, Sienna was acutely aware of Fox in the small room. She'd come here to make sure he was okay, but his presence pushed into every nook and cranny of the space and made it impossible to think clearly.

"We're not supposed to spend a lot of time in here though," she said. Her voice trembled slightly when she remembered the look Bruce had given them that first day. The look that implied they were never supposed to hide out in the safe room.

Fox sighed. "Yeah."

"So, let's head back into the woods. Get you some fresh air," Sienna said, pleased her voice sounded steady despite the excited thrumming of her heart.

Why did she have such a hard time controlling her emotions around him?

His smile grew and transformed his entire face. "That would be great."

*Oh yeah, that's why,* she realized with a twist of her stomach.

She grabbed his hand and pulled him out the door. Sienna told Bruce she'd try to get some good footage, and she would, but that didn't mean she wanted everything to be caught on camera. That would be something for later. Now, she just needed to get Fox out of here without getting noticed.

It surprised Sienna that the desire to be alone with Fox was stronger than the pull to shine onscreen. But maybe it was just because he actually liked her for who she was, when no one else seemed to. Even Audrey and Harper had given her a talking to before they started the table decorating, telling her she needed to tone it down.

Like she needed the reminder how over the top she was being. For every question Audrey had gotten right, Sienna had whooped like it was the winning shot at the state finals. Her victory dance when the boys had lost had been part drumline, part chicken dance.

But their comments hadn't been as painful as Fox's scowl from across the room. Its silent judgement of her phoniness had almost taken all the fun out of winning.

Sneaking out of the inn with Fox, however, was turning out to be a lot of fun.

He held her hand tightly in his as they made their way to the trailhead at the end of the long gravel driveway to the inn. Sienna didn't see cameras anywhere and prayed it would stay that way. She wanted Fox to open up to her again. She wanted to see the soft and kind version of Fox that made her heart race.

"What happened back there?" Sienna asked once they were safely under the green canopy of fir and spruce. Night was falling, but she'd grabbed a flashlight from the front desk on their way out.

He dropped her hand and ran it through hair. "Harry."

Sienna waited to see if there would be more, but Fox stayed silent.

"You let that jerk get you all riled up?"

"You didn't hear what he said about Reagan. He's such garbage. She deserves so much better. And he deserves a punch in the face."

"Why didn't you do it then? You seem strong enough to do some real damage." She flushed at the way the compliment sounded like she was drooling over him. Had that been too over the top?

"I *could* do some damage, that's why I left." Fox looked down at their feet, grabbing Sienna's hand to lead her over some rocks in the path.

Her heart fluttered at his unexpected touch.

"I've done a lot worse to people and told myself I never would again."

The air hung heavy with his revelation. Sienna swallowed hard. "What have you done to people?"

Fox pressed his lips together. For a long time, it didn't

seem like he was going to answer, but then he took a deep breath. "I told you about my ex and how she left. That wasn't really the end of my career. I could have recovered, but I let that pain destroy me. I lashed out at everyone around me. Most of the band stuck with me when Becky left, but I'd get into fights with them over dumb stuff. I would throw a punch at the smallest provocation."

He looked to the sky and breathed in through his nose.

Sienna squeezed his hand.

"I also started drinking and partying, way more than what you'd expect from a normal college kid," he said. "Which obviously didn't help the fighting. Within a few months, the label had dropped me, and everyone had left."

"Everyone but Eli?" Sienna asked. When Fox nodded, she started putting the pieces together. No wonder he was so loyal to his friend. Going on this ridiculous show must have been Fox's way of paying back Eli for his help years ago.

"Eli, Audrey, even Reagan, they were all there for me during the hardest year of my life. There's no way I would have survived without them."

"You're lucky to have so many people who care about you," said Sienna and stopped walking in front of a fallen log to sit down.

Fox stayed standing and shrugged. "A few people."

Sienna took a deep breath. "Well, you have one more now."

He looked down at her, brows furrowed. "What do you mean?"

Ugh, guys needed everything spelled out for them,

didn't they? "*I* care about you."

He folded his arms across his chest. "Me? The scowling grump?"

Sienna's lips curled up in a smile. "You're so much more than that."

He dropped his arms and looked down at his feet. "You're so much more than an attention-seeking phoney."

Sienna's heart went into overdrive. If only that were true. She *wanted* it to be true, but the cameras—and how to act in front of them—was always in the back of her mind.

Even now, she needed to tell Fox about Bruce and how she'd promised to give him some good footage for the show. Fox wouldn't like the idea of playing it up for the cameras, but maybe if he knew about the roles they were playing *before* they showed up, he wouldn't be so resistant. Especially if it was for Eli.

Just as she opened her mouth to tell him, he sat down next to her on the log. *Right* next to her. As in, no space whatsoever. Their legs were pressed together, and his hand settled somewhere on the log behind her back. Her senses were completely overwhelmed by him, and she instantly forgot whatever she was going to say.

She turned her head and looked up in his eyes. The night air was cool, but warmth flooded her and made it hard to breathe. She struggled to keep her breaths even, not wanting Fox to see how affected she was by him.

"Do you really care?" he asked softly, his words sending shivers down her spine when his breath touched her face. "Or is it just for the cameras? Because Bruce said we looked good together?"

"We *do* look good together," she said with a

slow smile.

He chuckled, and she could feel the rumble in his chest pressed against her side.

"But I do truly care. I didn't expect this to happen. It kind of ruins all my plans for kicking your butt in this competition."

At this, he threw his head back and laughed, the sound echoing into the dark night. "I have laughed more this week than I have in months," he said, and drew up his hand to brush it across her cheek. She closed her eyes, wanting to remember everything about this moment. "And I think it's because of one very annoying, very cute bridesmaid."

"Reagan?" She smirked but felt a tug at her heart.

"She's a friend." Fox smiled and relief flooded her veins. "A good one. But she's more like a sister after everything she's been through with me."

She smiled up at Fox. "Did Harper win you over with her amazing s'mores, then?"

He rolled his eyes playfully at her. "You're going to make me spell it out, aren't you?"

Sienna loved seeing this fun, flirty side of Fox. And seeing him like this made her relax. She was absolutely going to make him spell it out for her if that meant she would get to see more of it. She shook her head and lifted one shoulder. "I have no idea what you're talking about."

Fox closed his eyes and took a deep breath. "I'm having a good time, and I think a big part of that is you."

When Fox opened his eyes again, Sienna's breath caught in her chest. If playful Fox was fun, this smoldering version threatened to consume her.

Fox brushed a stray strand of hair out of Sienna's face, and let his fingers linger on her cheek. The tips of his fingers were rough against her skin, and Sienna leaned into his touch.

He closed the distance between them as his other hand reached out and gently wrapped around the back of her neck. Fox's gaze stayed glued to her the entire time, and Sienna suddenly felt the world shift.

*Oh my goodness,* Sienna thought. *He's going to kiss me.*

But that realization was nothing compared to the fact that she wanted to kiss him too. She licked her lips and held her breath. Was this really happening? How could someone so good, so loyal, feel this way about her?

Fox bent down, so close that their lips were almost touching and—

A loud sneeze broke through the clearing.

Fox and Sienna jumped apart from each other, and their heads snapped in the direction of the sound. There, crouching behind a small tree with a camera propped on his shoulder, was the cameraman from earlier. The red light was blinking, which meant he was filming.

It was suddenly very hard to breathe. Sienna wasn't sure if she was more upset about her kiss with Fox being interrupted, or the fact that they'd been caught. Either way, this was bad. Really bad.

What had she been thinking? She had been genuinely worried about Fox, otherwise she would have realized how naive she'd been when she didn't think the cameraman would follow her. Of course he followed her even when she told him to wait. If she thought she'd have an opportunity to warn Fox about getting more footage, she was living in a dream land. Now her thoughts raced as she tried to figure out the full extent of her carelessness. Maybe the cameraman had just started filming. Maybe he hadn't captured the entire very personal and very private conversation, or their almost kiss?

One look at Fox's face, and she knew it didn't matter what footage they'd gotten. His trust in her was completely shattered.

It wasn't like Sienna had planned for this to happen, but she knew how it must look to Fox. She turned to face him, to explain what was really going on, but his hard expression made her throat dry up.

"I'm an idiot," he said under his breath.

"No, you're not," Sienna said, finding her voice. "This isn't what you think."

"Oh yeah? And what do I think?"

Sienna's heart pounded. "That I brought the cameras up here deliberately. But I swear I didn't. I wanted time alone with you, away from them."

"Do you even like me? Or were you trying to make me kiss you for TV?"

"I wouldn't do that." She shook her head and reached out to him. "Trust me."

Fox pushed her hand away. "Funny, that sounds almost exactly like what Becky said when I first suspected she was going to ditch me."

Her stomach roiled. This was everything he was afraid of, and it was all her fault. "But this isn't the same," she said, her hands falling helplessly to her sides. He had to see that she really cared.

"You're right. It isn't the same because this time I'm not going to fall for it again."

## 7 Days Until Dream Wedding

H E WAS AN IDIOT.

This was exactly why Fox stuck to the small beach town he called home and worked on boats. Other than Eli and a handful of others, people always let him down. Becky, most of his college friends, and now, Sienna.

How dumb did he have to be to think that someone like her could change in three days?

She was a professional actress. Fox had seen her cozying up to Bruce and Jason, trying to get on their good side by doing whatever they wanted. Besides, Fox and Sienna were practically strangers. It was foolish to think that she would do a one-eighty and be authentic—for him, no less.

Fox ran his hands through his hair as he stormed back to the safe room. It was small, it was cramped, but it was better than Sienna and her lies—or the cameras. Thankfully, the cameraman had stayed behind with Sienna. She would need to do damage control for her image, no doubt.

And it was better that way.

Once inside the small storage room that doubled as the safe room, Fox let out a loud growl that bordered a scream. When that wasn't enough to satisfy the frustration flowing through his veins, he hit one of the shelves that held linens. Hard.

The entire shelf collapsed with a loud crash, and towels spilled across the floor.

The small space was trashed, and Fox struggled to catch his breath. It was too similar to the chaotic scenes from his post-Becky days.

Back then, he'd start drinking, let his temper get the best of him, and next thing he knew, something would be broken. He'd ruined all his relationships, other than his friendship with Eli, and caused so much self-destruction, he'd vowed never to let himself fall down that hole again.

And for ten years, he hadn't.

Fox pressed his palms against his eyes and focused on breathing—inhale, exhale. He was embarrassed that he'd lost control. And knowing that all it took was one of Sienna's lies proved he wasn't ready to open up to anyone. Not anytime soon, at least.

Once he was calmer, Fox opened his eyes and assessed the mess he'd made.

The white towels were scattered across the floor, but thankfully, there wasn't anything breakable mixed in with them. And once he kneeled down and examined the shelf he'd knocked off the wall, he discovered it wasn't actually broken. It was the kind that sat on brackets, and he had just knocked it out of place.

With one last sigh, Fox lifted the shelf and set it right. He looked down at the towels. He debated folding them and putting them back, but who knew the last time this floor had been cleaned.

He gathered the linens in a giant heap and walked out of the safe room, only to run into Wade and Eli. Fox thanked his lucky stars it wasn't Bruce or the cameramen.

Wade's wide-eyed gaze went to the giant pile of towels in Fox's arms, to Fox's face, and back again. "Hey buddy, what were you doing in there?"

Fox felt his face heat up. He could either let his friend's imagination run wild, or he could admit that he'd totally lost his cool. He closed his eyes. "I, uh, hit the wall and knocked the shelf over."

"Oh, Fox," Eli whispered.

When Fox opened his eyes, he was sure he would see disappointment on his best friend's face. Instead, he was met with a small smile.

"Here," Eli said as he reached out to grab some of the towels. "Let me help you."

"Thanks, man."

"I guess I should grab some too," Wade said with a sly smile. "But I'd better not find out you threw up in them."

Fox rolled his eyes. "They spent all of two minutes on the ground. Other than that, they should be fine."

"Cool," Wade said as he shifted the pile of towels in his arms. "Any idea where we're taking these?"

Fox pressed his lips together. "I think I saw a maid's station on the other side of the building. Want to try that first?"

"Sure," said Wade, and the three guys headed down the hall.

Fox didn't see any cameras, and while he was thankful for the temporary semblance of privacy, his senses were on high alert after what happened with Sienna. He was constantly looking over his shoulder and down halls.

Eli raised his brows at Fox. "Want to talk about what's going on?"

Fox grunted. "Not really."

"Okay," Eli said slowly. He was quiet for a beat longer. "Maybe you could start with why you were hitting things in the safe room."

Fox sighed. He really didn't want to talk about it. But Eli was his best friend, and when he'd gone down his dark path all those years ago, talking to Eli had helped him tremendously. "Sienna."

Wade laughed. "I knew you were going to end up falling for that girl."

*Falling? More like tumbling down the mountain onto a pile of jagged rocks.*

The entire thing had been a game to Sienna. While Fox was putting himself out there for the first time in ten years, she had been trying to get good ratings. And the worst part? Fox should have known better.

Sienna was leaving after the wedding, and Fox would go back to his boats. Things would never work between the two of them. And because of that, he didn't want to tell his friends just how much Sienna had hurt him. Fox returned Wade's eager, teasing smile with a glare.

Wade shifted the pile of towels once more and lifted a hand. "Fine. No one is falling for anyone," he said, but Fox couldn't help but notice the way a corner of Wade's mouth lifted as he said it.

Eli turned back to Fox. "But I'm still curious what this has to do with Sienna."

"I talked to her about Becky." He paused. "And everything that happened after."

Eli's eyes went wide. "You did?"

Fox nodded.

"She didn't take it well?" Eli asked, his eyebrows furrowed.

"No, that wasn't it." Fox opened his mouth to elaborate but spotted the door to the maid's station.

The three guys walked inside, much to the surprise of the staff, and explained what had happened. Fox apologized for giving them extra work to do when the show had already turned things upside down for them and was met with gracious smiles from the employees.

Once they were finished dropping off the towels and were back out in the hall, Eli stopped and put his hand on Fox's shoulder. "If it wasn't your past that freaked her out, what happened?"

Fox brushed Eli's hand off of him and started walking again. To where, he wasn't sure. Just as long as it was away from the cameras and Sienna.

"Dude," Eli said firmly as he jogged to catch up to Fox's quick pace. "What happened?"

Fox spun on his heel and faced them. He knew they'd just badger him endlessly until they got the whole story. So, he might as well get it over with. "She lied to me. She can't be trusted, just like Becky."

Eli's head recoiled. "Are you sure? That doesn't sound like the Sienna I know."

Fox snorted. "I mean, how well do you know her? She lives in York, right? You see her maybe twice a year for holidays?"

"Yeah, but—"

"Listen. I went to the safe room after what happened

with Harry. I needed to calm down for a couple of minutes. And guess who showed up? Sienna." He stopped and gave Eli a tight-lipped smile. "She pretended like she needed a break from the cameras too. Yeah, right, like she ever wants to be out of the spotlight."

"It's possible she needed a break too." Eli didn't sound too convinced.

*Possible, but not probable.*

"But that wasn't it," Fox said. "She pretended to care. We had this big heart to heart, and I thought I was getting to see the real Sienna and then—" He pursed his lips together. They didn't need to know about the almost kiss. With any luck, no one would ever know. "Then the cameraman, who had been hiding behind a tree the entire time, sneezed."

"Whoa," Wade said.

Fox pointed at him. "Exactly. It was all for show."

His friends both shook their heads and frowned.

"It really doesn't sound like her," said Eli. "I know she's kind of a drama queen but the past few days..." He bit his lip.

"What?" said Fox. "She's been magically transformed? Having cameras everywhere and the fame she wants most within reach have somehow made her less interested in the spotlight?"

"She hates this as much as you do, I know it." Eli crossed his arms. "She wants to be a real actress, not some reality show drama queen."

Fox snorted. "Well she's doing a really good impression of one."

"I don't know if she can fake the way she looks at you," said Wade, rubbing his chin. "When you two start fighting like bratty kids, it's entertaining for everyone, but her whole face lights up when you walk into a room."

Fox wanted that to be true, so badly. More than Eli or Wade could possibly understand. But could he really let himself trust so much after everything he'd been through?

"I can't think about all of this right now," he said and ran his hands through his hair. "I need a break. A real one."

Wade lifted a finger. "I know," he said. "How about we go out tonight. The next competition isn't until tomorrow. We'll find a way to *really* lose the cameras and get a drink or something."

A drink or something.

Wade was great, but he didn't know all of Fox's past, not like Eli. And while Fox didn't have a problem with other people drinking, he had done a good job of staying away from alcohol for the last ten years. After his fit in the safe room earlier, he didn't think it was a good idea to go anywhere near a bar.

But escaping the Emerald Inn sounded great. Escaping the cameras even better.

He nodded. "Let's do it. Let me just grab my hoodie real quick."

But when Fox turned to go up the stairs to his room, he saw Sienna racing down the hall toward the safe room—and there were tears in her eyes.

## SIXTEEN

## 7 Days Until Dream Wedding

---

SIENNA RUSHED to the safe room. She wasn't sure how much Bruce had seen—or how much had been captured on camera—but regardless, things were not going well.

*Please let it be empty, please let it be empty.*

She opened the door, and relief flooded her veins when she found it vacant. She hurried in, closed the door and leaned her back against it. The tears that were already spilling down her cheeks began to fall in thick streams as Sienna struggled to catch her breath.

The last hour had been a nightmare in every possible way.

First, there was the look of utter betrayal on Fox's face when the cameraman sneezed. The two of them had been about to kiss, something Sienna didn't even know how much she wanted until then. But when Fox realized he'd been set up—not that Sienna had done it on purpose—he thought it was for all for show.

Second, there was the way the cameraman walked up to her afterwards to get a close up of her reaction. Even with her years of acting classes, Sienna wasn't sure she'd covered up the gut-wrenching agony that had torn through her body at the sight of Fox running off down the path.

She'd tried to storm off like Fox had but unfortunately the cameraman stayed right behind her the entire time. As they walked toward the Emerald Inn, he'd asked questions like, "How long have you guys been sneaking off to make out?" and "Do your sisters know?"

But the pièce de résistance, the fishhook in her heart, had been "Do you think Fox will ever talk to you again?"

Sienna knew he was trying to get footage of her breaking down. His job was to pester her with difficult questions while emotions were running wild. But she didn't have answers for his questions and hadn't been able to say a word without risking the tears building in the corners of her eyes from spilling over.

Then there was the fact that her roommate had sent twenty-three texts in the time it took to get down to the inn. Sienna had quickly glanced at each one, careful not to let the cameraman see what was on the screen. Each message was only a few words, and misspelled at that.

*Where are u?*
*Landlord keeps calling...*
*I need a check by tmorrow.*
*Or our boxes r on the street.*

Sienna was in trouble and there was no way out.

And last, but not least, Bruce was waiting for her when she finally arrived at the Emerald Inn. He wore a smile the size of Texas when he saw Sienna and asked for an interview about what happened with Fox.

That had been the final straw.

While she couldn't be sure, since her vision was blurred from the tears that fell, Sienna thought she might have seen Bruce's impossibly wide grin grow even further at the sight of her emotional breakdown.

She raced through the inn, not caring who she bumped into on the way. She just knew she needed to be someplace away from Bruce, or Jason, or the cameramen who seemed to be everywhere.

Sienna sank to the floor, her back still against the door of the safe room, as she pulled out her phone.

*Seriously? Lila sent* three *more texts?*

She didn't bother reading them. Instead, she quickly dialed Lila and put the phone to her ear. It didn't even get a chance to ring before the voice of her roommate blared through the speakers.

"Look who finally decided to call me back," came Lila's angry voice.

"I've been busy."

"Oh, that's right. With that reality show for your sister's wedding." A tired sigh came through the receiver. "Did you get your big break yet?"

Bruce's smile filled Sienna's mind again, and she struggled to compose herself. She didn't need Lila knowing just how dire things were. They were friends, and they'd helped each other out when some months had been tight, but this time they were both overdrawn and out of time.

"I'm really close."

"That's really great, and I'm happy for you and everything, but that doesn't change our current problem of a very irritated landlord. He said he's let late rent slide too many times. He needs dependable tenants."

"I know—"

"Which is why I've started accepting applications for sub-letters."

Sienna's breath caught in her chest. They'd always talked about taking on a third roommate, under the table, of course, but leaving the apartment had never been an option. It couldn't be. Not when they were both so close to making it. "You what?"

Lila paused, and Sienna's heart sank. "And I've already found someone I like. They can move in two weeks. It'll take all the pressure off both of us."

Easy for Lila to say. She'd still have a place to live when the new girl moved in. What was Sienna supposed to do? All of her fears of coming home with her tail between her legs were coming true.

"What about my stuff?" she managed to squeak out.

"The new girl moves in after you get back from North Carolina. That should give you at least two days to pack."

Sienna bit the inside of her cheek to keep the tears at bay. She wasn't sure if she should be relieved Lila wasn't throwing her stuff in the front yard.

"Okay."

"I'm sorry," Lila said, her voice softer now. "But I can't risk losing the apartment because I can't cover the full rent. If it had been the other way around, and you'd needed to get someone last minute, I wouldn't be mad at you."

Sienna nodded, even though Lila couldn't see—and even though she would never do the same thing to Lila.

"I'll see you when you get back, okay?"

Sienna nodded again and ended the call.

The sobs that burst out of her shook her entire frame. She didn't know what she was going to do. One thing was for sure, she never wanted to leave the safe room.

Sienna looked around the small space. Other than one completely empty shelf, the room was stocked with enough linens to make a small bed. Maybe if she put enough blankets under her, the floor wouldn't be so bad.

A soft knock came on the door.

She sniffed. "Occupied."

"Sienna?"

It was Fox.

Sienna groaned and covered her face with her hands. And as much as she wanted to talk to him, Sienna didn't want Fox to see her like this either.

"Can I come in?"

"What is it with you and bothering me when I'm in locked rooms?"

Fox didn't answer, and she'd thought he'd left, until the sound of his soft command came through the door.

"Let me in."

Sienna had lost all her willpower to refuse him. With a deep breath, she stood up and opened the door. She peeked over Fox's shoulder to see if anyone else was waiting outside. Bruce was standing down the hall with his arms crossed, but there weren't any cameras nearby. The producer raised his brows at her, but she ignored him and stepped aside to let Fox inside the small closet.

"Is everything okay?" Fox asked once he closed the door behind him.

No, everything most definitely was *not* okay. And even without knowing all the things that had happened to Sienna since they parted ways, it should have been obvious to Fox. Mascara must be streaking down her face and her eyes had to be red and puffy.

Sienna snorted. "Yep. Everything is just peachy, thanks for asking."

Fox fixed her with a stare.

Sienna crossed her arms over her chest. "Why are you here? Don't you hate me right now?"

"Eli said you hate this reality show thing as much as me. Is that true?"

Great, now the boys were gossiping about her? She hoped Bruce hadn't been around to hear it. Sienna could not deal with this right now.

She shrugged. "Does it matter? You've already made up your mind about me."

"Just answer the question."

Boy was he annoying, even when he had every right to be mad at her.

"Fine, I hate it. Happy? This isn't what I trained for. This isn't what I want to do. But it's the only way to get me where I need to go."

"Is that why you're crying?" He took a step closer. "What's going on?"

A desire to tell him everything warred with her need to keep up her facade, even if it was mascara-covered and puffy. "It's not your concern."

Fox took another step closer, putting his body only inches from hers. Her traitorous eyes went to his mouth as her mind drifted to the almost kiss.

When Sienna managed to drag her eyes back to Fox's, she noticed that he was also looking at her lips. So, she wasn't the only one who was thinking about what had happened in the woods. Sienna shoved down the flutter of hope that idea prompted in her heart. She cleared her throat, and Fox's cheeks turned red.

He shook his head. "I just want to help. Maybe there's a way to shut down this whole crazy show.

Audrey and Eli won't want to keep going if we're both miserable."

*Both miserable?*

Apparently, he *wasn't* thinking about kissing her. He'd come to his conclusions about Sienna, and he was desperate to get away from her. So desperate, he was trying to shut down the entire show.

But maybe it was better this way. Things were messy enough without their feelings getting involved. If they could go back to hating each other it would be easier to finish filming this stupid show and make sure Audrey and Eli got their dream wedding.

Sienna crossed her arms over her chest. "I don't need your help. I don't need some kind of knight in shining armor. And even if I did, you're obviously not the one to rescue me."

When Fox recoiled, Sienna knew she'd gone too far. But really, what was Fox going to do? Pay her rent? Convince Lila to let her stay? Maybe he could use his musical influence to get her a role in the next big sitcom.

Yeah, right.

Fox ran a hand through his hair. "It's okay to need help sometimes."

She shook her head. "I don't."

"You don't have to pretend to be perfect."

Pretend to be perfect? Sienna felt anything but perfect. Things were starting to unravel left and right, and now Fox wanted to come into the safe space and remind her that she wasn't good enough? No way.

"I know I'm not perfect." She gave him a tight-lipped smile usually reserved for over sharers on the subway. "But thank you so much for pointing that out."

"That's not—"

"My mother is always telling me how I'm not doing great in York and how I should just come home. But thank you so much for the extra support."

"I just want to help."

"Well, you trying to fix my problems isn't going to change the mistakes you made in your past." Unwilling to let him see the tears that were building fall, she threw open the door to the safe room and stormed out.

She barely registered the sound of the door closing behind her as she stepped into the hall and the strong stench of cologne hit her. With a sinking dread that at least served to dry up her tears, Sienna remembered that Bruce had been lurking outside the safe room.

She gave him a wary look. He was waiting for her, but she had no more energy left to pretend she was happy. And if that meant looking miserable for the camera, so be it. But if he wanted to get some footage of them talking about what happened in the woods, where were the cameras?

Bruce marched over to where she lingered just outside the safe room. His face was stern as he grabbed her by the arm and dragged her to a small office down the hall. *This can't be good*, she thought when he closed the door behind him and spun to face her.

"What do you think I meant when I told you I needed some footage of you and Fox?" His eyes were blazing.

Sienna flinched at his tone but kept her chin up. She could fix this. "That you needed footage of us?"

"Oh, good. So, I was clear. Then would you care to explain why you tried to lose my cameraman when the two of you went into the woods?"

Her heart almost stopped. "I didn't."

Bruce lifted his brows.

"I mean, it wasn't like that." She held up her hands in front of her. "I was trying to talk to Fox so we could figure out how to give you something good."

He pinched the bridge of his nose. "I know everyone thinks reality TV is scripted, and maybe that's why you thought you needed to *do* something. But I needed real footage of you and Fox."

"And there's real footage of us in the woods," Sienna said. Horrible, damaging, painful footage of Fox and Sienna opening up to one another followed by Sienna's apparent betrayal. Meaning, reality show gold. Bruce should be thrilled right now.

"I need more than that. I needed to capture that kiss. And if you couldn't give me that, I should have gotten your roommate drama."

Sienna's stomach dropped to the floor.

"Yes, I could hear all about how your roommate is going to kick you out and *that* was my something good. Too bad you made it impossible for me to use it by hiding out in the safe room."

"But that doesn't have anything to do with the wedding."

Bruce threw up his hands. "Who cares?"

Sienna cared. All of that drama with Lila was personal. It was beyond embarrassing, and it would paint Sienna in the worst possible light. She would look like an irresponsible and naive little girl who couldn't hack it in the big city. The cameras didn't see her working sixty hours a week on top of auditioning all over the city.

"People love a good wedding," Bruce said, his words slow and biting. "But they also want all the skeletons in everyone's closets. Viewers want to see the people on TV fall apart, and then pat themselves on the back for being so much better than them."

"But—"

"And you might think you're special because you're an 'actress' just like every other twenty-something with a pretty face, but you're not."

But she was more than just a pretty face. Sienna wasn't looking to get by on her looks alone. She'd worked her butt off for every single role she'd gotten. Her mother's words about how sometimes working hard wasn't enough echoed in her mind.

And though Sienna wasn't sure she had any more tears to shed, she felt the tell-tale sting behind her eyes.

"Don't try to lose my cameramen again, understand? Or else."

Sienna nodded as Bruce walked out of the office and left her alone once more.

*I'm an idiot,* she thought as she paced back and forth in the small room.

All this time, she thought she'd been getting on Bruce's good side. All his and Jason's comments about how well she was doing had to have meant something.

Who was she kidding? Helping out a struggling actor wasn't Bruce's priority, or even something he liked to do. He was in the business of making viewers happy, not helping a 'twenty-something with a pretty face' get a job.

And did he mean it when he said, "or else?" Did he mean taking legal action? What would happen to Sienna and her family if he followed through on that threat?

While Harry worked at his father's law firm, Sienna wasn't sure he'd be willing to defend her, or anyone in their family, if push came to shove. Harry cared about Harry. And, in his weird, harsh way, Reagan as well.

This meant she would need to be extra good from here on out. No more letting Lila drama distract her. No more trying to open up to Fox and be his friend. Sienna needed to keep her eye on the prize.

And warn her sisters.

## 7 Days Until Dream Wedding

---

SIENNA HURRIED to the second floor and knocked loudly on Audrey and Harper's door. "I need to talk to you."

The door flew open to reveal Audrey, makeup-free and in her pajamas—and she looked ticked off.

"What do you want?" Her sister's tone stung, but this was important.

Sienna looked up and down the hall. "Can I come in?"

Audrey huffed. "I guess."

Sienna rushed inside and closed the door behind her. "Are Harper and Reagan here?"

"No." Audrey shook her head. "Harper had to run down to Flour Girl and take care of some business stuff, and Reagan is off somewhere with Harry."

Sienna bit her lip. She really hated the idea of having to tell this story multiple times. It was embarrassing and painful, and Sienna would have much preferred ripping it off once like a Band-Aid. But she couldn't wait. Audrey needed to know.

She bounced on the balls of her feet. "Listen. I made Bruce mad."

"What?"

Sienna hurried to explain everything—how Bruce had pulled her aside and asked for her help, how she'd been caught on camera talking to Fox, and the way Bruce had threatened Sienna with, well, she didn't know exactly, but it couldn't be good, could it?

The only thing she left out was the drama with Lila.

When Sienna was done, her sister stared at her with an unnatural calm. All the air seemed to drain out of Sienna's lungs. The lack of emotion on Audrey's face was worse than if she was yelling at her.

"This is great." Audrey threw up her hands and plopped down on her bed. "Just great. As if things could get any worse."

*Get any worse?*

Sienna thought everyone was having fun competing against the boys and being out in the mountains. It had been a welcome break from the stress of her life in New York until the craziness of today had thrown everything off-kilter.

But maybe she wasn't the only one hiding her worries behind a fake smile.

She took a step closer to Audrey. "Is everything okay?"

Audrey dropped head into her hands and sighed. "No. Everything isn't okay. Eli and I had a huge fight."

A fight didn't sound too bad. "I'm so sorry, but I'm sure it's just nerves. When you're not used to being 'on' all the time, it can be draining for people."

Audrey glared at her. "You don't have to bring up

your acting career in every conversation, Sienna. Not everything is about you."

Ouch. That stung. Sienna took a deep breath and brought her focus back to her reason for coming: warning Audrey that the whole wedding may be in danger. This wasn't about her, this was about everyone. But first, Audrey clearly was dealing with something, and Sienna wanted to help.

"What happened with Eli?"

Her sister shook her head. "I don't want to talk about it. I just want to go to bed."

Another deep breath kept Sienna from saying something rude. She was exhausted and looking for comfort, too, and had thought she'd be getting it from her sister. Now she had to deal with two crises.

"You don't have to tell me about Eli, but what should we do about Bruce?"

Audrey's face went scarlet. "We? I've been doing everything right, Sienna. You're the one that went rogue and decided to make this the Sienna and Fox show."

"But you said that he…" Sienna swallowed hard to keep the tears prickling at her eyes from falling. "You and Harper and Reagan made me think that…" She shook her head.

"If I had known you'd blow up the entire show because of some silly crush, then I wouldn't have teased you so much about him. Or told you all that personal stuff."

"It's not a silly crush, I—" Sienna stopped. What, exactly, did she feel for Fox?

Audrey sighed, long and deep and tired, and rubbed her temples. Sienna's heart dropped. That was the classic end-of-her-rope Audrey move. Even her students knew when the temple rubbing started, that they were really in for it.

"Look, we're both tired," said Audrey. "If you could just try to make it through the next few days without adding more drama or making this somehow about you, that would be great."

Sienna opened her mouth to say something, but the words never came.

"Why don't you go back to your room and try to stay out of trouble. I'll see you at breakfast." Audrey walked over to the door and opened it. She stood standing next to it in silence waiting for Sienna to leave.

"Yeah, okay," Sienna said as she walked out into the hall.

The door immediately closed behind her.

How had everything gone so terribly wrong so quickly? This morning, Sienna had a place to live, was looking forward to her sister's wedding, and was eager to see what would happen with the thing building between her and Fox.

Now, she just wanted everything to be over.

———

FOX WAS DONE. They weren't even halfway through filming, and it was just too much. Sienna had gotten under his skin in every possible way, and now all he wanted to do was escape. He needed a way out, a way to break that stupid twenty-page contract, to get back to the safety of his boats, far from the confusing mess his heart and head were in right now.

He needed to find Harry. As much as the guy made his skin crawl, he was a lawyer. Hopefully a good enough one to get Fox out of the show without messing anything up for Eli and Audrey.

When Fox came out of the safe room, Wade was waiting for him. "Ready to head out?"

Fox wavered. Going out didn't mean he had to drink anything, right? It would be a way to escape, for sure. One he had managed to avoid for years. And Harry would be around when he got back from wherever Wade planned on taking him.

"Let's go."

Sneaking out of the inn unseen by the cameras was no easy feat. Members of the crew were stationed by the tent they had set up around the front of the inn to keep some of their equipment. The two pulled up their hoods and walked toward the parking lot.

"Just need to grab a CD from my car for the awesome playlist we're making for the wedding," shouted Wade in the direction of the tent. Softer, he said to Fox, "Hopefully something as boring as that won't draw their attention."

"That's ridiculous. Who has a CD player in their car anymore?" whispered Fox as his heart pounded in his ears.

They weren't supposed to go off the property unless it was for the show, though Harper had a little more freedom because of her bakery. Heading out now was breaking at least one, possibly two, of the clauses in the contract.

Fox looked around. "Where's Eli?" He suddenly realized the groom-to-be was nowhere in sight. "Waiting for us in the getaway car?"

Wade shook his head. "He said he needed to talk to Harry about something."

A flicker of hope shot through Fox's body. Maybe by the time they got back, it wouldn't even matter that they'd broken the contract. Maybe it would be null and void anyway. Fox had meant what he'd said to Sienna. There was no way Eli and Audrey would continue if it was making all their friends miserable.

Thinking about Sienna sent a burning flicker of pain through Fox's heart. He'd been beyond furious at her betrayal in the woods, but what if Eli had been right, and she really hadn't meant it? Fox's brain had told him to look at the evidence, but his heart had wanted to give her a second chance.

Except when he'd given her that chance, she'd lashed out at him in the meanest possible way. All he'd tried to do was help, and she'd thrown it back in his face.

No, he was done thinking about her. Done thinking about anything other than getting out of the Emerald Inn for the night.

They were finally at Wade's car, but instead of opening the door, he pulled Fox down behind it, so they were out of sight from everyone. "You still run an eight-minute mile?"

Fox raised an eyebrow. "Why?"

"We can make it to the highway in fifteen if you can keep up. From there it's a quick rideshare away from town."

And with that, Wade bolted through the parking lot, careful to crouch behind the cars as he circled along the edge. Fox hesitated for the briefest of moments before he followed, looking back only once to see if anyone had noticed. There was a flurry of activity at the entrance to the inn, and Fox picked up his pace. He caught up with

Wade and flew past him down the long sloping drive to the inn.

After leaving the parking lot and making the long jog to the highway, they'd hid in the bushes at the end of the drive, to see if anyone was following them. Sure enough, five minutes later, two white production vans made their way down the long winding road that led to the inn. One went left and the other right.

Wade called a car, and it was an anxious eight-minute wait and ten-minute drive before they made it to downtown Wellspring. Once there, they played a game of hide and seek with the white vans through town. Wade and Fox ducked into stores whenever a car passed them on the street, then ran as fast as possible down the sidewalk.

Fox felt the thrill that only breaking the rules could give him. And in the grand scheme of things, these weren't such terribly important rules to break. He hadn't hurt anyone or stolen anything or broken any laws. This was the familiar exhilaration of youthful depravity, and he'd forgotten just how sweet it could be.

For the first time in what felt like years, though it had only been four days, Fox felt free.

———

THEY ARRIVED at the bar sweaty and out of breath, and the two friends took the booth the farthest from the door. The fruity smell of hops permeated the air.

"I'll grab you a coke?" Wade was standing, halfway turned toward the bar.

Fox felt the country music pounding in his ears, and the rough, squeaky vinyl against his sweaty skin. It was a simple question with a simple answer. But the fire of rebellion had been lit inside by their escape from the inn.

"Rum and coke," Fox said.

Wade frowned. "You sure?"

Fox took a deep breath and looked his friend in the eyes. "Yeah."

Wade spent the next thirty minutes talking about everything and nothing, while Fox's drink sat untouched in front of him, sweating beads of condensation onto its cardboard coaster. While Wade prattled on, Fox watched the ice slowly melt to the sound of his heart hammering in his ears.

"Dude, have you been listening at all?" Wade waved his hand in front of Fox's face. "You gonna drink that or just stare at it all night?"

"I..." Fox looked up at his friend, and down at the watery rum and coke sitting in front of him. The air was suddenly too noisy, too thick, and he was having trouble breathing. "I have to go."

Fox shot out of his seat before Wade could even open his mouth. Back outside in the cool North Carolina night, he took off down the street in the direction of the Flour Girl Bakery. It wasn't because he wanted to see Harper—he didn't want to see anybody right now—but it was in the opposite direction from the inn. By now, anyone out looking for them had most likely given up the search.

This was not how Fox thought this night would go. Just a few short hours ago, when he'd been in the woods with Sienna, it had felt like the beginning of something.

But what, exactly?

It had been so many years since he'd let himself feel

this much that it had taken him completely by surprise. His teasing had shifted at some point during the past few days from a place of annoyance to a place of attraction. Sienna had let him see past the fake smiling facade, and he'd fallen for the soft, beautiful, caring girl hiding behind it. He knew that she could be better, could be so much more than what she was showing people.

Could he accept both parts of her, knowing that her dreams depended on her keeping that facade in place?

Or would saying yes to whatever was happening with Sienna have the same effect as saying yes to a drink? It could take him down a familiar, shameful spiral, scraping bottom all because he let his feelings for someone else cloud his judgement.

There was no way to know.

So he had to do what he'd been doing so well the past ten years: protect himself. The risk was just too great, and he'd already lost so much. Sure, giving Sienna another chance and letting his heart call the shots might lead to something amazing, but it could also blow up in his face. So, he had to stay away.

It was the only way to be sure.

## EIGHTEEN

## 6 Days Until Dream Wedding

If it weren't for her need for coffee, Sienna would have stayed in bed all day—all week even. She had no desire to go downstairs or see anyone. Audrey. Bruce. Fox. They were all sources of pain, in their own unique ways.

But the bright sunlight on her face reminded her that it was a new day, and no matter what kinds of new pain it might bring her, she would need caffeine to face them. So Sienna pulled on her cutest pair of jeans and ran a brush through her hair. Then she put on the smile she'd spent hours in front of the mirror practicing and went downstairs.

The quiet and subdued mood in the dining room was a surprise. Voices were low and it was like the energy had been zapped out of everyone.

Sienna looked around in a panic, but her heart rate slowed when she saw that both Audrey and Eli were in the room. They weren't sitting at the same table, but at least they were here.

Sienna was still too hurt from what Audrey had

said last night to go over and talk to her sister—especially since she was at a table with their mother—but she was still happy that, for now, the wedding appeared to still be moving forward. She didn't want Audrey to be unhappy just because she was mad at her.

Sienna grabbed a large cup of life-giving java and plopped down next to Harper and Reagan just as Bruce came up to the front of the room.

"Good morning, everyone." His smile was wide, but his eyes were dark. "I think we're all feeling the pressure of shooting on such a tight schedule, so I wanted to tell you all how great you're doing."

Sienna's stomach twisted, and not just from the way Bruce looked at everyone in the room. She'd need food soon, not just coffee, if she was going to get through today without bailing.

"It appears that you all need a break, so instead of shooting the next competition this morning, we'll shift it to the afternoon. Enjoy a quiet morning, but make sure to stay on the Emerald Inn's property. In a few hours, we'll meet back here, hopefully refreshed."

"Well that was nice of him," said Sienna, her eyes wide. After the way he scolded her outside the safe room, she was surprised that he was being so compassionate.

Harper and Reagan, however, looked skeptical.

"Not really," said Harper. "He's hoping we'll all walk around the woods talking about what happened last night."

"What happened?" The panic was back in Sienna's veins, making her as jittery as if she'd had three cups of coffee instead of one. Her head spun around, and she realized that Fox was not in the room. Had something happened after she'd run off?

"Fox and Wade escaped into town." The corner Harper's lip twitched up. "They said they were getting something from his car and then just ran down the mountain. A rideshare picked them up at some point, and they hid out in a bar."

The coffee sloshing around in Sienna's stomach threatened to come right back up. Fox had run away because of her. He'd been worried about her, but she'd made him feel bad about everything, even when she'd been the one at fault yesterday. She'd pushed him to the edge and look where he'd ended up.

"How do you know all that?" Sienna asked.

Harper's cheeks flushed pink. "I was down at the bakery last night dealing with a delivery issue," she said, not quite meeting Sienna's eyes. "I had a camera guy with me at first, though who knows what an hour of footage of me sorting through inventory will do for the show. But then he got a call and was picked up by one of the production vans. I knew something big must be happening but didn't know what until I saw Fox an hour later wandering the streets on my way back."

"Wandering...Drunk?" Sienna felt the shame wash over her. This was all her fault. He'd told her about his destructive past, and she'd pushed him anyway.

Harper shook her head. "Just tired, I think. He didn't talk much on the way back but told me all about his and Wade's daring escape."

Reagan snickered into her cup of tea, but Sienna didn't see what was so funny.

"How could they have just run off like that?" Sienna

clutched her coffee mug. "We're not supposed to go anywhere. What about the contract?"

"It'll be fine. Don't worry about it," said Reagan, putting her hand on top of Sienna's. "They just needed a break. So now we all get one. Be happy. We can go back to our rooms and do a face mask or something."

Pampering and forgetting about everything else? Sienna's desire to sit around and do nothing warred with the one to find Fox and make sure he was okay.

Reagan smiled up at her, giving Sienna pleading puppy-dog eyes. And though Sienna still wanted to make sure Fox was okay, she also had heard, first-hand, the way Harry had been talking to Reagan since they all arrived at the Emerald Inn.

She sighed. "I'll meet you in your room in ten?"

Reagan nodded.

Sienna turned to Harper. "You coming too?"

Harper was looking around the room, however, not at her sister. "Um, I think I'll pass. A walk outside does sound nice."

Sienna's stomach clenched. She'd already messed things up so much with Bruce, and she didn't want to see her sister fall for his tricks too. She imagined all the great footage they could get if Harper wasn't careful. "You're not going to talk about last night with anyone are you?"

Harper shook her head. "I'll just be walking around by myself. And if anyone asks about what happened, I'll just explain that Fox called me for a ride back to the inn last night. Super boring. It won't make for good TV."

"And hopefully bridesmaids putting on facial masks won't either," said Reagan, with a glance at Bruce. "Let's go."

TEN MINUTES LATER, Sienna was seated on the chaise lounge in Reagan's room, cucumber slices on her eyes, and the cool wetness of a hydrating blend of aloe and snail mucus on her skin.

She let out a long, low sigh. "This was a great idea. I really needed to relax."

"Me too," said Reagan from her spot on her bed. She'd kept her eyes cucumber-free in order to flip through a bridal magazine. Sienna could hear her turning pages and the scratch of her pen as she took notes.

"Getting ideas for your own big day?" asked Sienna.

What she really wanted to ask was why Harry was still here after what she'd overheard in the forest, but frankly, Sienna's own drama was enough for the morning. It was better to focus on fun things like weddings that wouldn't involve eight cameras and a cranky producer.

"Yeah…" Reagan's voice drifted off. "I don't know when it'll happen, so I can't really do much until I know what season to plan for."

"When do you think you'll set a date?"

"Harry really wants to make partner first before we make any plans." Reagan flipped a few more pages. "He's under a lot of stress right now at work."

"It's great that he could take the time off to be here," said Sienna. She was heading into dangerous territory, but Reagan had left that one wide open. Maybe talking her through it would take Sienna's mind off her own stuff. "He'll be able to stay until the end?"

"I—" Reagan stopped.

Sienna peeled off one of the cucumbers to peek at her friend's face that had turned a bright scarlet.

"Right now, that's the plan. I'll let you know if anything changes."

"Yeah, there's been quite enough changes lately."

"Oh?" Reagan's eyebrow raised.

Sienna popped the cucumber back on her eyelid to avoid her inquisitive stare.

"Changes, like feelings have changed?" Reagan asked.

More like Sienna had arrived with an apartment and now she had none. She was still too embarrassed to tell anyone that she was officially homeless, though she'd have to tell her mother soon enough if she hoped to live with her until she figured things out.

But Reagan wasn't entirely off base when she assumed Sienna was talking about feelings. Sienna's emotions had been all over the place since she met Fox, and while he hadn't come out and said it, she knew he felt something too. Though after how she'd left things last night, those feelings weren't the warm and gooey kind anymore.

"I don't know what you're talking about," Sienna mumbled.

"You've totally flipped since our first day. You were all gung-ho, this is about my career, and now you're hiding from the perfect opportunity to get on camera? What on earth has happened in the past four days?"

Sienna felt the trickle of a tear beneath her sheet mask and pulled it off, along with the cucumbers. She ran to the bathroom to throw it all in the trash then grabbed the tissue box on the back of the toilet. In the mirror she caught sight of the goopy mess of her face and the tears started to pour out of her.

Reagan was beside her in an instant. "Oh, sweetie, what's the matter? Is this all because of what happened yesterday?"

"Wh-which part of yesterday?" Sienna blubbered. The energy drained from her completely, and she sat down on the floor of the bathroom. "The part where I accidentally betrayed Fox, or the part where I yelled at him on purpose for trying to help me? Maybe it was the part where Bruce is mad at me for not getting good footage with Fox?"

"I'm sure it's not as bad as all that," said Reagan, and she put her arms around Sienna's trembling shoulders. "Bruce seems to have gotten the message we're not his typical group of attention-crazy celebrity wannabes."

Sienna choked out a laugh. "Except that's exactly what I am."

"Not from what I've seen. You may have one of the best fake smiles I've ever seen, and you were a little over the top that first day, but you're trying to do what's best for Audrey and Eli, and I think everyone can see that."

Sienna sniffed. "Thank you."

"And as for the Fox problem, he got a break last night. I'm sure he's in a better mood today. It can all get sorted out. You just need to talk to him."

If Sienna talked to Fox, she would have to explain what was going on. Her heart rate quickened. "I can't."

"Of course you can. We all lose our cool from time to time."

Sienna shook her head. "No, it's not that. He can't

know why I was hiding in the safe room in the first place."

"And why were you in the safe room?" Reagan asked, her brow furrowed.

Sienna blew her nose in a raspberry so loud that she was sure the cameras downstairs would be able to hear, but she didn't care about stuff like that right now, not when she had so many other things to worry about. "I've been trying so hard to make it work in New York, but I just can't afford it anymore. My roommate found someone else to take my room. When I go back after this, it's to get my stuff, and that's it for me. My dream of being an actor is officially over."

The relief of finally saying it out loud to someone was like breaking a faucet, and it all gushed out of her. Reagan held her while she cried in long, racking sobs for what felt like hours.

When the tears had slowed to a steady trickle, Sienna looked up at Reagan. "I didn't want anyone to know. I wanted you all to think I had it figured out."

Reagan crinkled her forehead. "Why on earth would you want that?"

"Because you all have it together. I've always been the kid sister that everyone takes care of. Even you; it's like I had three older sisters. I want to be a grown woman who can take care of herself, just like you all can. I don't want any of you to worry about me."

"You think we all have it figured out?" Reagan started to laugh, softly at first, then louder.

*It's not* that *funny,* Sienna thought. But then again, Sienna had never heard Reagan laugh this hard, so there had to be something she was missing. That, or Reagan had finally cracked.

"We have no clue what we're doing," she said through lingering chuckles. "We're all figuring this adulting thing out as we go."

"But if I can't do it on my own, if I'm not perfect then—" Sienna stopped and bit her lip. She'd already told Reagan about her apartment, but this was something else.

"Then what? The world will end?" Reagan stopped laughing and gave Sienna a small, sad smile. "That kind of pressure comes from crazy pageant moms like mine, not like nice, normal ladies like Emily Hudson."

"I know it won't." Sienna frowned. "I'm just thinking about Milo."

Reagan's eyebrows shot up. "You've heard from him?"

Sienna shook her head. "No, but Dad left when I was little because I was too much. Three kids, fine, but four, and a crazy attention-seeking toddler like me..."

"What does that have to do with Milo?"

"Well, Milo did the same thing, just ten years later. I was too much for him. I'm too much for everyone. I need to show them that I can do it on my own, that they won't have to take care of me. Then no one else will leave."

"Oh, Sienna." Reagan sighed and took her hands in hers and knelt in front of her to look her in the eye. "You had nothing to do with anyone leaving. I don't know much about your dad, but I do know there is nothing a three-year-old could do to make her father leave."

The faucet of tears that had started to twist off was back on full blast now. Sienna breathed in Reagan's words, wanting them to be true, needing them to be true.

"And I only knew Milo a little, but from all the stories your sisters and Eli have told me, he was loyal to a fault—especially to his family. It must have been something beyond his control to pull him away from you all."

It made sense, hearing it from Reagan. Sienna had told herself that hundreds of times and never believed it. But after everything that had happened in the past few days, anything seemed possible. Her entire life felt like a reality show, with one dramatic surprise coming after another, so maybe she could suspend belief a little more and accept that what Reagan said was true.

"So what am I supposed to do?"

"Be you. Just you, however you want to be," said Reagan, giving her a hug.

"But I'm an actor. I'm never just me."

"Well, start now. It's reality TV, after all."

Sienna sighed and wiped her eyes. It seemed like they'd stay dry for at least a few minutes. "We don't have anything until the competition this afternoon. Should we just stay here and try another mask?

"Actually, I think you should talk to your mom."

"That charcoal one looked good—"

"Sienna." Reagan leveled her with a stare eerily like Audrey's irritated teacher look. At least she wasn't rubbing her temples. "You need to tell her about the money problem. Maybe she can help."

Sienna snorted. "She can't wait to tell me 'I told you so,' you mean."

"I highly doubt that. And if she does, then you never have to listen to my advice again."

## 6 Days Until Dream Wedding

FOX WOKE up to the sound of knocking.

He laid in bed for several moments waiting for the fog of sleep to fade. And as it did, his mind began to come into focus.

There was someone outside his room.

The sun was shining through the thick curtains just enough that Fox could tell that it was late morning.

*Late morning?*

Fox shot up in his bed and snatched the phone off of his dresser and saw that it was already past nine. He'd slept through that morning's meeting—that morning's *required* meeting.

Fox jumped out of bed and hurried to get dressed. He was pulling his shirt on over his head when a voice cried out from the other side of the door.

"I know you're in there, so you might as well open up, buttercup."

It was Wade. Better than Bruce.

Still, Fox was late, and wasn't sure what kind of competition they were supposed to be starting right now.

He glanced at the small bathroom in his room and debated giving his teeth a quick once-over before answering.

Fox shook his head. He was already in hot water after last night. So, with one last longing glance toward his toothbrush, he answered the door instead.

On the other side was a much-too-refreshed looking Wade. He wore a giant smile on his face and carried two cups of coffee. "Everyone was wondering where you were."

Fox grabbed the extra coffee from Wade's hand and hurried to explain. "I forgot to set my alarm when I got in last night, and these stupid curtains make it so the sun doesn't come through the windows, and—"

Wade's chuckle cut him off. "Relax. You're good. Bruce gave us the morning off."

Fox's head whipped up. "He what?"

Wade smiled. "I guess he sees how hard all of this has been on everyone and wanted to give us a break."

Fox's mind was sharp from the adrenaline of his jumpstarted wakeup, and the idea of Bruce giving them a break just didn't feel right. Bruce didn't do anything out of concern for the contestants on *Wedding Games*. Fox knew that much, at least. But he'd get to brush his teeth after all. He waved Wade in and ushered him to the small chair in the corner of the room.

"So why do you think he's giving us a break?" he asked before he loaded up his toothbrush and started brushing.

"Who knows why that guy does anything that he does?"

*Ratings,* Fox thought as he moved on to flossing.

"He told us to enjoy the property, and I thought I

might go for a walk to loosen up my muscles after last night," Wade said. "My quads are feeling tight."

Now that the initial panic of messing things up for Eli and Audrey had passed, Fox could feel all the aches and pains that came from the previous night. While his work kept him healthy enough, Fox wasn't eighteen anymore. His body wasn't prepared for the late-night mountain run, or the secret agent moves through Wellspring. He was acutely aware of his lack of sleep thanks to the way his mind had buzzed with thoughts of Sienna until 4 a.m.

And he was *still* thinking about her.

Fox nodded. "Sure. Sounds good."

He grabbed a pair of tennis shoes, and five minutes later, Wade and Fox were walking along one of the various hiking trails surrounding the Emerald Inn.

"So, where's Eli this morning?" Fox asked once the massive building was out of view. It was unfortunate the camera still followed just a few yards behind them.

Wade gave the cameraman a quick glance. "He's, uh, in the safe room with Audrey."

Fox's eyebrows shot up.

"Everything's fine." With a high arch to his eyebrows, Wade jerked his head toward the camera.

Whatever Eli and Audrey were doing, Wade didn't want to say on camera. He continued to make weird faces, but Fox couldn't interpret what Wade was trying to say. They needed a distraction, or to lose the camera-man, but even then, Fox knew better than anyone it wasn't foolproof. Just because you didn't see the camera, didn't mean it wasn't there.

"So, how about the Bears," he said, hoping his slight hesitation wasn't noticeable.

Fox didn't know anything about football, but it seemed like a safe—and boring—topic of conversation. With any luck, Wade and Fox could be so bland, the cameras would want to leave.

A corner of Wade's mouth tipped up. Apparently, he was much better at playing charades than Fox. Wade started rattling off statistics and droning on about this player and that coach and their chances at making it to the Super Bowl this year. The words came out so smoothly, like Wade was an expert, though Fox wasn't sure if any of it was true.

Fox nodded and made sounds of agreement as Wade continued, but the cameras were still there. He was just about to give up hope that he'd be able to talk openly with Wade, when the cameraman's phone rang. Fox held his breath as he listened to half of the conversation.

"Yeah. Uh-huh. Nope, just sports talk. Yep. Be right there."

The guy didn't even bother saying goodbye to Fox and Wade before going down the trail back to the inn.

The two friends watched his retreat in silence, and at some point, Fox realized he was holding his breath. Once the crew member disappeared behind some trees in the distance, Wade started laughing.

Wade patted Fox's back hard. "I knew you were hopeless, but seriously, I started listing the Weasley family tree once it was obvious neither you nor the cameraman were paying attention."

Fox looked up with a sheepish smile. "Yeah, not my thing."

"We can't all be perfect like me."

"Perfect." Fox rolled his eyes. "But now that he's gone, what's going on with Eli and Audrey?"

Wade glanced around the woods, like he expected someone to jump out any second. Honestly, Fox wasn't convinced they wouldn't. But he looked at Wade expectantly anyway.

"Audrey wants to stop filming."

"Are you serious?"

Wade nodded.

"That's great." Though not entirely unexpected. Fox thought this might happen. "There's already been so much drama, and we're not even halfway through this crazy thing."

"Yeah." Wade scratched his beard. "It would be great, except the contract states that the production company gets to keep the footage they already have."

"So what?"

Wade sighed. "Can you imagine how angry Bruce would be if we all just up and left? What do you think they'd do with what they have?"

Fox wasn't sure, but Wade made an excellent point. Enough had happened in the last few days, that they could easily twist it into something juicy if they wanted.

"Not only that," Wade said. "Audrey and Eli have already put a down-payment on a house."

Another revelation Fox wished he'd known about sooner. "That might have been a little premature."

Wade shrugged. "No kidding, but you know how it is." He punched Fox on the shoulder and winked. "When you find the right one, you just gotta go for it."

Like Wade was one to talk.

While Wade was a nice guy, he still wasn't the kind of guy to settle down. Fox couldn't remember a single time in the past ten years when Wade had had a serious girlfriend or long-term relationship.

Fox snorted. "Oh yeah? And what do you know about going for it?"

"You know I don't kiss and tell." A sly smile crossed his lips. "Actually, I think this is the perfect question for you though."

Unease filled Fox's veins. "What do you mean?"

"Don't play dumb." Wade shook his head. "Have you decided if you're going to go for it with her?"

Fox didn't need to ask who *her* was. *She* was hovering at the back of every thought Fox had had in the past twenty-four hours.

"You know that I can't."

Wade stepped over a small creek that was flowing down the incline of the mountain they were hiking up. "Sienna's not worth it?"

Fox sighed. "She's totally worth it. But I don't know if she thinks it is."

"But you've already said you think she is. So, what's the problem?" Wade asked.

"You know, I could fall head over heels for her, bare my freaking soul to her, and then she could leave me to my self-destructive ways."

"You're describing what happened with Becky."

"Yes, but I'm also describing what happened yesterday with Sienna."

"You're not having much luck with the ladies, are you?" Wade laughed.

Fox shot him a hard look.

Wade lifted his hands in surrender. "Look, I know Becky was the worst thing that could happen to a guy. She was selfish and greedy and narcissistic. But we're not talking about her. We're talking about Sienna."

Fox shook his head and brushed some branches out of his way. "It doesn't matter who we're talking about. Anyone is capable of doing horrible things to someone else."

"Sure, they might be capable of it. But does your gut tell you that Sienna is going to do that?"

"She's got this personality that comes out when the cameras are around and—"

"And you're worried Sienna is going to somehow use that TV personality against you?" Wade interrupted. "Do you think she's out to hurt you the way Becky was?"

Their feet rustled through the leaves and branches on the path. Fox thought about the moments he'd shared with Sienna. That first day, she'd acted immature and only allowed him to see the persona she adopted whenever Bruce and the cameras were around.

She put on a bright smile because she took her role as bridesmaid seriously. She wanted Audrey and Eli to have a great wedding and knew how to play the game. She'd spent years cultivating this persona and was using it to her advantage.

That didn't mean the girl he saw in the stolen moments wasn't genuine. In the days that followed Fox's first impression, he'd seen glimpses of the girl—woman —she was beneath that facade. A woman who listened to Fox when he opened up about his past. A woman who didn't judge him for it. A woman who loved her family fiercely. A woman who was determined and worked hard.

"I'm guessing by your expression, you don't think

Sienna is out to get you," Wade said, pulling Fox from his thoughts.

He smiled. "No, I don't think she's out to get me. I actually think she's pretty incredible."

"And how do you feel?" Wade asked. He grabbed a tree to steady himself as they hit a steep decline in the path.

There was a slight singsong quality to Wade's tone that he knew made Fox uncomfortable. And it worked. The question made Fox feel even cheesier about the direction his thoughts had turned.

"I feel like...I've never felt like this before." Fox stopped at the bottom of the decline and looked back up the hill. Luckily the trails were well marked because he had been paying zero attention to where they were going. "But what about everything that's happened? Maybe I should just let her go."

"Is that what you want?"

Fox shook his head. "No, the thought of never seeing her again after *Wedding Games* makes me feel sick."

The grin on Wade's face grew. "And what are you going to do about it?"

Fox shoved him off the trail and into a bush. "I don't know yet." All he knew was that he had to do something big, and soon, before they went their separate ways.

Wade stood up and brushed the dirt off his pants. He smacked Fox's back. "Good. And now that that's settled, let's head back down to the inn. This walk is only making my muscles feel worse."

Fox said a silent thank you. His body was also protesting after last night's rendezvous, but he hadn't wanted to say anything. "Sounds like a plan."

TWENTY

6 Days Until Dream Wedding

___________

Sienna paced outside her mother's room.

The parents of the bride and groom were set up in a different wing of the Emerald Inn, and Sienna had avoided that part of the giant building like the plague —until now.

After Reagan refused to let her do another facial mask—using the annoyingly convincing argument that it would do more harm than good to her complexion— Sienna had retreated to her room.

She knew it was a bad idea to go anywhere that the cameras would be until that night's competition. They could technically come into their rooms at any time, but there were only so many cameras, and Sienna hoped the drama was unfolding elsewhere at the moment.

Watching Sienna lay on her bed and sort out the tangle of her thoughts would not make for the most scintillating television.

Her mind jumped from Lila and the apartment, to Fox and the argument they'd had, then to the pressure of *Wedding Games* to Milo. Everything bounced around inside her head until she couldn't take it anymore.

Sienna had told herself that she *wasn't* going to talk to her mother, but inevitably, her feet had taken her there anyway. She still didn't know what she was going to say, so she stayed in the hall threatening to wear a groove in the floor from her back and forth.

She could have kept it up indefinitely, but the door swung open and her mother's head appeared in the doorway.

"Are you planning on staying out there all morning? Or did you want something?"

Sienna's face heated, and she considered telling her mother that this was all part of her new exercise routine. "I-I was wondering if maybe you'd want to talk?"

"Sure. Let me just get my room key, and we can go downstairs for some coffee."

"Actually." Sienna forced her face into a smile. "I was thinking we could hang out in your room?"

A small line formed between her mother's brows for the briefest moment before she nodded.

Sienna looked down the hall to see if there were any cameramen ready to follow her but didn't see any. She crossed her fingers it would stay that way.

Sienna stepped into her mother's room and all thoughts of being filmed vanished. This room was *nice*. It was roomier than the ones given to the bridesmaids. It was even bigger than Audrey's, and she was the bride, for crying out loud. There was a Jacuzzi tub sitting under a giant window that overlooked the wooded property.

Sienna whistled low. "Wow. They really set you up, didn't they?"

Her mother lifted a single shoulder. "Did they? I wouldn't know since none of my girls have invited me to their rooms since we got here."

A pang of guilt ran through Sienna. She'd been so caught up in everything going on that she hadn't considered that her mother would want to see her room. And it sounded like Audrey and Harper had been as thoughtless too.

"Well, I can promise you that you're not missing anything. My room faces the parking lot, and my bed is a twin, not a king-sized one like yours. And I have a shower stall, nothing nearly as cool as this," Sienna said, waving her hand at the tub. It was much easier to talk about her mother's room than the difficult things that still hummed in the back of her mind.

A small smile touched her mother's lips. "It is pretty amazing."

"Tell me you've poured yourself a glass of wine, used bubble bath, and taken advantage of this gorgeous view."

Her mother nodded. "Every night."

Sienna groaned. "That sounds amazing."

"It is." Her mother paused. "But I have a feeling you didn't come all the way over here to talk about my room since you didn't even know what it looked like until now."

Sienna closed her eyes. "No, I didn't."

"Do you want to tell me why you're really here, then?"

*No. Not really,* she thought, but opened her eyes and nodded.

Sienna sat down on the edge of the bed, and her mother perched next to her. The silence that stretched between them was like a tiny hole that was pulled bigger and bigger with each passing second. Her mother sat patiently, her hands folded one on top of the other, while Sienna wiped her sweaty hands several times against her thighs.

Why was this so hard? It was her mother. Her mother loved her. Nothing bad would happen if she admitted her mistakes, right?

Just utter humiliation and shame, no big deal.

Sienna took a deep breath. "I lost my apartment."

Her mother opened her mouth, but Sienna pushed on. To hear any criticism before she'd gotten it all out would crush her, and she'd never be able to finish. She told her mother everything—her three jobs, Lila's ultimatum before she came to North Carolina, her fed-up landlord, how she had to pack her things and find a new place to live.

When she was done, her mother took Sienna's hands. "Oh, honey. I'm so sorry."

Sienna's chest tightened, waiting for the other shoe to drop. "But..."

Her mother frowned. "But what?"

"But 'I told you so,' obviously."

She shook her head. "Is that really what you expect me to say right now?"

"Yeah. I know you've been waiting for me to fail as an actor and now you get to tell me how you were right all along."

"Oh, Sienna." Her mother leaned over and pulled her into a tight hug. "I've never wanted to see you fail as an actor."

Sienna wiggled out of her mother's grip. "Of course you have. That's why you're always telling me how I shouldn't be working all these extra jobs and should just come home."

Her mother's eyes watered. "I'm so sorry that's the impression I've given you. I'm so proud of all that you're doing."

These were pretty words, but they didn't make sense. They were in total opposition to everything she'd ever heard from her mother. She folded her arms across her chest. "And when you told me that hard work isn't always enough?"

Her mother reached out to grab Sienna's hand. This time she didn't pull away. "I don't want to see you work away your youth. I've had to make a lot of sacrifices for you girls."

"Exactly, and——"

"And they have been joyful sacrifices, done out of love. But I want better for you girls. It's why I co-signed on Harper's bakery and gave her a small gift to help with the startup costs."

Sienna's mouth dropped open. "You what?"

"You thought she was able to start Flour Girl on her own a year out of college?"

Sienna nodded.

"Well, she wasn't." Her mother smiled a little. "She needed help. And so did Audrey, when she wanted to get her master's in teaching."

All of this was news to Sienna. In the last couple of hours, her entire world had been twisted upside down, and she wasn't sure what to think anymore. "Does that mean if I had asked for help, you would have given it?"

"Of course I would have. I want you girls to do your best, and you've always been so stubborn when it comes to admitting you're not able to do things on your own."

"I wonder who set that example for us?" She tried not to sound bitter.

"I had no choice but to do it on my own. The example I tried to set was that it's important not to blindly rely on a man to take care of everything. But sometimes people need help, and that's okay."

Warmth rushed through Sienna's body. She'd felt so proud of doing it on her own, but it felt even better to know she wasn't alone when it really mattered.

"And I'm still happy to help. All you need to do is ask."

"Even now?"

Her mother rolled her eyes. "Yes, even now. I worked hard so that I could save up a bit. Not enough for Audrey's dream wedding, unfortunately, but enough to help out in a pinch."

"I wish I'd known."

Her mother squeezed her shoulders. "Well, now you do. Do you want to call Lila and tell her you have rent money and want to stay?"

Sienna frowned. Lila had already chosen someone to replace her. Sienna didn't want someone else to end up without a place to stay because she'd been too stubborn to tell her mother about what was going on.

She shook her head. "No, I think it might be too late for that."

"Are you sure?" Her mother shifted in her seat to take hold of Sienna's hands and look her in the eyes. "Like I said, I have it tucked away for emergencies."

"Yeah," Sienna said. "But maybe you can help me with the deposit and come up to help me pick out a new place?"

Her mother smiled widely. Sienna's hotel room

wasn't the only place she'd never invited her mother to visit. "Absolutely." There was a long pause before she added, "Anything else you want to talk about?"

Sienna shook her head. "I don't think so."

"Not even Fox?" Her mother wiggled her eyebrows.

"How do you—" Sienna cleared her throat. "I mean, what are you talking about?"

"Just because I haven't dated since your father left, doesn't mean I'm blind. And that Fox sure is a handsome one."

"Mother!" Sienna's eyes went wide.

"I'm just saying it looks like there's something going on between you two. I may not be competing in all these silly games, but I've been around. I see the way he looks at you. And more importantly, the way you look at him."

Sienna shook her head. "Not anymore."

"What do you mean?"

"He's pretty mad." She leaned back in her seat and sighed.

"And does he have a right to be?"

"Yes. No. I don't know." Sienna buried her face in her hands. "He thinks I did something bad, but it was an accident."

Her mother clasped her hands in front of her. "That's even better. You can just go to him and explain what happened."

Sienna let out a short laugh. "I don't think it's that easy." She'd escaped utter humiliation and shame this time, but wouldn't be so lucky with Fox.

"Of course it is."

Oh, how Sienna wished it was as simple as her mother thought. But it wasn't. If there was only a way to make her understand…

She sat up straight. "What about Dad?"

Her mother narrowed her eyes. "What about him?"

"After he betrayed you and left, what would you have done if he came back and explained that it was a misunderstanding? Would you have forgiven him? Would you have listened?"

Her mother bit her bottom lip. "I don't know. But I doubt whatever you did was as bad as him leaving me and four kids without warning."

"It's not. But it's still a big deal to Fox. And I doubt he'll even want to listen to me now."

Sienna closed her eyes and willed the tears that were forming in her eyes to stop, until she felt a comforting hand on her shoulder. She opened her eyes and took in her mother's sad smile.

"He might not listen, but do you think it's worth a shot?"

Sienna honestly didn't know, but she doubted it. It was probably better to reach down deep in her acting arsenal and wear a bright smile for the next six days. Then Audrey and Eli could get married, Sienna could find a new place in New York, and Fox could go back to his life, far away from her.

She looked up at her mother with a sad smile of her own. "I don't think so."

## TWENTY-ONE

## 6 Days Until Dream Wedding

Taking a risk had sounded easy enough when Fox was on the trail with Wade, surrounded by the dark green canopy that made his heart rate slow and his mind clear. Now, under the glare of lights and critical eye of three cameramen, Fox felt the familiar itch to run up to his room and hide. He took a deep breath and tried to concentrate on what Jason Castle was saying.

"Welcome to the final challenge." Jason smiled at them all.

They were in the same meeting room as the first day, set up to look like a church again. Fox tried unsuccessfully to ignore the urge to peek over at Sienna standing with her sisters on the other side of the room. But even without turning his head, he knew Audrey was happily sitting with the bridesmaids, and Eli was back with the groomsmen.

For better or worse, they had decided to continue on with the show.

"To recap, we have the bride's team in the lead. They won the s'mores contest and will get to select the menu. They also won the scavenger hunt, so they'll be choosing the flowers. And—thank goodness—they won the table decorating contest so ladies, you'll be picking your own dresses."

The girls laughed, and Fox allowed himself to sneak a glance in their direction as they all ran their hands over their foreheads in an exaggerated show of relief. Apparently, having people walk out in the middle of the table decorating competition hadn't affected the end result. Or maybe they'd just edit the footage so that it wasn't even apparent anyone was missing.

A shiver went up Fox's spine when he thought of Wade's words. Even if everything stopped today, Bruce could still do whatever he wanted with the footage they'd already taken. Would Fox come out as a nice guy or as a total jerk after disappearing? The one way to be sure was to keep playing along and doing what was expected of him.

"The groom's team won the obstacle course and the right to play whatever music they want on the big day." Jason turned his megawatt smile on the guys. "And maybe today's competition will give you some ideas."

How could today's competition give them ideas unless it was musical? Fox's stomach clenched.

*Please don't let it be...*

"I hope you all like karaoke!"

Fox let out a groan that was thankfully covered up by the excited squeals from the girls. They were really going all in, not that Fox expected any less from Sienna. Even though she'd been upset the last time he saw her, he knew she'd put on a brave face and do her best for Audrey.

And Fox wasn't about to back down from his plan to

tell Sienna how he felt about her. And even though he hated karaoke, and there were cameras everywhere, Fox could use this challenge to his advantage. At least singing was something he was good at. And there were dozens of songs that worked great to let a girl know how you really feel. The hardest part would be picking the perfect song, with the perfect lyrics.

"Since this competition will decide who gets to pick the cake, all the songs should be about desserts."

*How much cheesier could this possibly get?*

"You'll be doing a group performance, so let's see those great coordinated dance moves."

A lot cheesier, apparently.

"The Wellspring high school drama department has provided some great costumes, so get creative."

Fox was ready to bolt out the door. This had to be a joke.

"You'll have one hour to pick three songs from the list and rehearse your choreography."

With a clap of Jason's hands, they were dismissed— and Fox's resolve wavered slightly.

He grabbed Eli's arm on their way out the door and to their assigned practice areas. "Singing and dancing in costume? Really?" he whispered furiously.

"Come on, it'll be fun," said Wade, coming to slap him on the back. "Just like when you performed in college, right?"

Fox raised an incredulous eyebrow. "Not quite."

He remembered his first open mic night, and the weight of his guitar strap on his shoulder as he looked into the dimly lit smoky bar. Pretty much the exact opposite of singing karaoke on reality television.

While dancing.

In costume.

The memory of that first performance also featured Becky, front and center at a table in front of the stage. Her eyes had shone with tears as he sang the song he'd written for her after their first date. Remembering how that moment of elation had led to so much heartache, Fox suddenly found it hard to breathe.

Maybe he wouldn't be able to do this after all—not even for Sienna.

"I can't do this," Fox said. The guys were walking toward the barn where a clothing rack was waiting for them. The sequins and beads on the various items glistened in the sun.

"After this it's all wedding prep stuff, and you won't have to be there," Eli said, his voice low. They didn't have mic packs yet and the cameras were still getting set up. "Please, Audrey is stressed out enough. Harry is refusing to help if anything goes south, and our offer on the house just got accepted. I just need this last effort from you."

"Can I just get a few minutes to clear my head?" Fox ran his hands through his hair.

Eli waved his hand in the direction of the trail behind the barn. "Be back in ten or I'm picking the songs without you."

Needing no other motivation than that to get back on time, Fox practically bolted for the safety of the woods. His shoulders instantly relaxed as soon as he stepped into the trees, and the sounds of everyone's voices faded away.

He didn't have to do the whole Sienna thing now, he told himself. He could wait until it was all over and see how things went the rest of the week. There was sure to be another opportunity to show her how he felt. Besides, she'd made it pretty clear how she felt about him when she'd called him a knight in shining armor. A big fancy declaration in front of everyone could end up falling flat. Taking that risk privately, where no cameras could capture his humiliation, seemed like the right choice.

Fox took a deep breath and let it out. He still didn't know what he was going to do, but at least he knew that it wouldn't be today. He had time to figure this out.

Deciding to at least take in the view Eli had shown him earlier this week before heading back, Fox turned the final corner in the path toward the ridge.

And ran right into Sienna.

———

"WHAT ARE YOU DOING HERE?"

Fox's angry voice cut straight to Sienna's heart. She'd come out here for a few minutes of peace before diving into the ridiculous embarrassment that would be her singing and dancing with her sisters. Hopefully Reagan, the former beauty queen, had some tricks to getting them all synchronized in record time, because Sienna had zero ideas.

And zero clue what to say to Fox's frowning face.

"Nice to see you too, grumpy."

A corner of his turned down mouth twitched. Maybe they could pretend yesterday hadn't happened, and she was still the annoying drama queen while he was the grumpy grandpa.

"Shouldn't you be rehearsing?" he asked.

"Shouldn't you?"

Sienna felt an odd satisfaction at the pink that tinged the apples of Fox's cheeks.

"I needed a break," Fox said, and Sienna's heart nearly broke at the sad look that descended on his face.

"Last night wasn't enough of a break?" She winced at how harsh her words sounded. Apparently she only had two modes with Fox: pouring her heart out or teasing meanness. Neither was appropriate at this moment, and she struggled to rein her emotions in.

"Who told you?"

"Harper."

Fox leaned against a tree and crossed his arms. "It was just some stupid fun. Not my best moment."

*All because of me.* The guilt in Sienna's chest was an inescapable tightness that threatened to consume her. So, she changed topics. "Today should be fun, at least."

He raised an eyebrow and his frown deepened. "This last competition is not what I was expecting."

"You don't want to sing?" Sienna would have been thrilled if they'd have been asked to put on a skit or play or something. She was also secretly dying to hear Fox sing again. She couldn't get the memory of his voice out of her mind ever since she caught him singing in the woods.

"Not like this, when it doesn't mean anything."

"It means something to Audrey and Eli."

He sighed and ran a hand through his hair. Judging by its unruly state, he had been doing that a lot during his walk. "When I sing—I mean, when I used to sing—it was to say something I couldn't with words. It was to make people feel something."

Sienna's breath hitched. "And karaoke doesn't make anyone feel anything except ridiculous?"

His lips twitched again, and a flutter of hope in Sienna's chest gave her the courage to say the words she'd been mulling over during her walk.

"I'm sorry."

His head snapped up, and a line appeared in between his eyebrows.

"I know, not what you'd expect from me, right?" Sienna gave a weak chuckle and flipped her hair over her shoulder. But that movement felt too playful for what she was about to say. She straightened her posture but felt too stiff.

Since when did she have a hard time acting the part? Since Fox. She didn't want to act around him anymore. She wanted to be herself. The *real* Sienna.

Sienna took a deep breath. "I'm sorry I didn't tell you we had cameras following us yesterday. I thought I'd avoided them, but clearly they're smarter than me."

"You're smart." Fox's voice was so soft Sienna wasn't even sure he'd spoken.

"For an actor, right?" She chuckled again, trying to bring forced levity to the situation once again. "I'm also sorry for what I said in the safe room. Just, you know, a blanket sorry for everything that happened yesterday."

"Everything?" The quirk of his eyebrow just about melted her right there in the middle of the forest. Was he thinking about their almost kiss?

Her heart sped up, and she decided to ignore the flutters the memory gave her. "I've been having room-mate issues. Money issues, really. And it turns out I need to find a new place to live."

He opened his mouth, probably to make some snarky comment about how immature she was, so she kept talking to avoid hearing it.

"Which is totally not your problem, and not something you need to or want to help with, but I just thought you should know why I was so mean. And I'm sorry, again, for being mean. You were just trying to help, but it's all taken care of, my mother and I talked, and everything is fine now so I'll be good the rest of the week, and I won't bother you anymore."

He snapped his mouth shut and blinked a few times once she was done with her long-winded babbling, and Sienna felt the heat rise to her cheeks. She looked at the ground and counted breaths in and out, waiting to see if he had any response.

When she got to fifteen, she looked up. He was staring at her with a mixture of curiosity and something else that she couldn't quite place.

"You don't have to say anything," she said, her face heating again. "I know you don't feel the same way I do, not after what I did, but—"

"How do you feel?" He tilted his head. "Besides sorry?"

Oh goodness, did she have to spell it out for him? Well, she'd already made a total fool of herself.

"I really, really like you," she said, her throat suddenly going dry. She swallowed hard, twice. "I don't —I don't know what exactly this is, or was, but I had hoped..." She trailed off and shook her head. "It doesn't matter. You don't feel the same, and I totally understand. It's fine."

She turned to head back down the trail. A hand on her arm stopped her. With a deep breath, she cleared emotion from her face and looked back at him, ready for whatever he was going to say. It would crush her heart, no matter what, but he was a nice enough guy to do it gently, at least.

"Sienna—" He glanced down at the watch on his wrist and dropped her arm. "I have to go."

And with that, he ran away, taking a piece of her heart with him.

## TWENTY-TWO

## 6 Days Until Dream Wedding

---

STAGE FRIGHT WAS NOT something Fox had ever really experienced.

He'd been in front of big crowds without even breaking a sweat. The music was so much a part of him that it usually couldn't wait to get out. Before shows he would be buzzing backstage, eager and ready to sing and play for as long as they'd let him.

So why was he a nervous wreck about performing in front of twenty people?

"Fox, buddy, you okay?" Eli slapped a hand on his shoulder, and Fox jumped as if he'd been electrocuted. Eli laughed. "Nervous?"

"A little." They were all milling around outside the meeting room, waiting for the crew to tell them they could go in. Fox crossed his fingers that some electrical malfunction would keep them outside forever.

"That doesn't sound like you." Eli crossed his arms and leaned against the wall.

Fox frowned. "Well, neither does this love song about candy we have to sing."

What he'd told Sienna in the woods had been true—he used his songs to say what his words couldn't. Eli didn't know that, so he couldn't know how frustrating it was to put on a performance like this. Even now, after everything, Sienna managed to get him to open up in ways he hadn't in years.

But the most surprising thing from their brief interaction had to be her apology. Completely unexpected, rambling, and insanely adorable. And it was obvious she had meant every rambling word with all her heart. A heart that apparently belonged to him, despite everything that had happened and everything he'd told her.

And he'd just stood there. The perfect, quiet moment he'd been hoping for, no cameras around, to tell her he wanted to give it a shot, to reassure her that he still felt the same, still wanted to see where this would go. But everything had hit him all at once, and so deeply, he'd been unable to say a single word.

So, he'd gone back to meet the guys and rehearse the ridiculous dance number with Eli and Wade. If nothing else, he didn't want Eli to have to eat an almond truffle cake infused with lavender and poppy seeds at his wedding. The fire he'd felt earlier in the week to beat Sienna had completely fizzled out, and his loyalty to Eli took over to keep him motivated.

And it was going to take a lot of motivation to get through this.

The meeting room had been transformed into a small concert hall. There was a guy manning the karaoke machine off to the side and a disco ball hanging from the ceiling. The group of judges sat front and center to the makeshift stage that Jason Castle was currently standing on.

"Alright, alright," he said. "It's time to see what you guys are made of. The bridesmaids won the last challenge, which means they got to choose who goes first. Drumroll please."

Jason turned to the DJ—not that you could call him that—and nodded his head. With a push of a button, a track of a drumroll started playing through the small room. "First up, the groomsmen."

Fox groaned as Audrey and her bridesmaids burst out in laughter.

Of course they chose the guys to go first. And from their perspective, it *was* funny. There was no way for them to know how hard this was for Fox. He tried to calm his frantic heart, and all of the guys—minus Harry, who said there was no way he was wearing those ridiculous costumes and making a fool of himself—made their way to the stage.

Thankfully, Jason nor Bruce made any mention of the missing groomsman, and with any luck, his absence wouldn't affect Audrey and Eli's wedding. Fox could only hope the same could be said for the secret performance Fox had planned.

Fox hadn't told anyone about the details of his plan to woo Sienna. He was too afraid they would talk him out of it. And Fox knew he would look for any excuse not to bare his soul on reality TV. The only reason he could follow through was knowing it would mean so much to Sienna. Or, at least he hoped it would. It was entirely possible Fox completely misread the situation.

Jason reached out and put a hand on Eli's shoulder. "So, what do you guys have in store for us tonight?"

Eli's mouth stretched into a large grin. "We're going to sing 'The Sweetest Thing' by U2."

"Sounds like a great choice. Good luck."

Eli thanked Jason as he exited the small stage, and the music started playing through the speakers.

Eli, Wade, and Fox all rushed to the back of the stage where they had stashed their costumes. Eli had the bright idea of dressing like the guys from U2 in the music video. Since Fox was uncomfortable, he got to hide behind dark sunglasses and a black cowboy hat, while Wade decided he would be all the random people in the background and had about ten costume changes. Meanwhile, Eli kept his Bono impression simple and wore a fedora and frameless glasses.

When they returned to the front of the stage in their new digs, the girls all squealed in delight.

Audrey clapped her hands and yelled Eli's name as he began belting out the ballad. Wade danced wildly from side to side, while Fox managed to get away with a lame, swaying back and forth move.

When Eli had finished singing the final note, Jason ran back on stage. "I must say, I'm impressed, Eli. Let's see what the judges have to say."

Fox held his breath as the judges held up signs similar to the Olympics. The groomsmen got a couple of eights and a nine.

"Looks like that risk paid off," Jason said once the scores were tallied. "What do you have next for us?"

Eli opened his mouth to say "Pour Some Sugar on Me"—another dessert-based song, though the lyrics were questionable—but before he could get a word out, Fox rushed over and pushed himself between Jason and Eli.

His heart pounded in his ears, and his palms were

sweaty. He took a steadying breath and smiled at Jason. "Actually, I'd like to sing a solo, if that's okay."

Eli leaned in and whispered, "What are you doing?"

Fox shook his head and glanced at Wade. "When you know, you know. And I think it's time for me to put myself out there."

A line formed between Eli's brows, but thankfully, a grinning Wade pulled Eli aside and whispered in his ear.

Satisfied that Wade would explain everything to Eli, Fox looked over to the DJ and nodded. He'd snuck in just before everyone was supposed to gather inside the meeting room and asked if he could be ready to play a song for him when the moment was right. And it had only taken Fox slipping the DJ a couple of bills to make it happen.

Fox only hoped that the guy manning the equipment knew this was the moment he'd paid him for. He walked up to the microphone, looked Sienna directly in the eyes, but didn't say anything.

Instead, Fox then put on a giant pair of rhinestone sunglasses and waited for the music to start playing through the speakers.

Fox didn't have a lot; he worked on boat motors for a living. But music was his passion and was what he could give Sienna. Even though they were someone else's lyrics, Elton John's "Your Song" said everything Fox wanted to.

He ignored the pit that formed in his stomach as the lyrics appeared on the small screen in front of him. He gripped the microphone as if it were the only thing keeping him upright as he sang the first line.

Once he did, everything else faded away. The stage fright, the cameras, even Wade and his stupid, knowing grin. There was only Sienna, and she was sitting perfectly still as she stared back up at Fox.

When his voice cracked, he hoped Sienna could hear the emotion he was putting into every word. He hoped she knew that he wasn't mad about what had happened. But most importantly, he hoped she could see that this was him telling her that he cared about her, and it didn't matter that all ten million viewers knew.

But Sienna hadn't moved a muscle, and Fox felt a creep of panic start in his stomach and reach up through his throat. He swallowed hard to loosen it up and put everything he had left behind the swell of the chorus and the words he felt with his whole heart.

When Fox finished singing the last note, and the music stopped, there was complete and total silence. Fox was breathless and the adrenaline pumping through him left a haze around his vision.

*This was a huge mistake.*

Suddenly, everyone burst into applause. Jason rushed back on stage, but frustratingly, Sienna stayed glued to her seat.

Jason patted Fox on the back. "Wow, someone give this guy a record deal! You've got a great voice. Let's hear what the judges have to say."

Just like before, the judges held up signs with a numeric score on them. A couple of sevens and a couple of eights.

Jason shook his head. "Tough crowd. But just so we know, why did you score Fox's performance lower than the group's?"

A young man from the hotel staff was the first to speak. "Well, he didn't really dress up. He only put on a pair of ugly sunglasses. And then, like, the song doesn't have anything to do with dessert or anything."

"Good points." Jason nodded. "And what do you think about that, Fox?"

Fox shrugged. "I don't."

"What do you mean?"

Fox focused on Sienna, whose eyes were glued to his. "I only care about what *she* thinks."

Everyone in the room turned to Sienna. Her expression didn't change much, but the tips of her ears turned a tiny bit red. Fox's heart sputtered. This was a mistake. She didn't want this.

"Why don't you come up here?" Jason asked with a dramatic wave of his hand.

Sienna slowly stood up and walked to the stage. But she didn't hurry to Fox, instead she stood on the other side of Jason. This was looking worse and worse for Fox. He inched closer to the edge of the stage, just in case he had to make a run for it to keep from experiencing the total humiliation of rejection on camera.

"Did you know Fox was going to sing this song for you tonight?" Jason asked. Fox held his breath.

Sienna shook her head. "No."

"And what would you give him as a score for his performance?"

Her eyes panned from Jason to Fox to the cameras. A slow smile spread across her face. Did that mean she wasn't going to reject him after all? Fox wasn't sure, but he'd had enough. He'd just done one of the hardest things he'd done in ten years, and he needed to finish this conversation with Sienna privately.

He reached out and grabbed her hand. When she looked up at him, he jerked his head ever so slightly to the exit doors. Her smile grew as understanding dawned, and she gave him a small nod.

Fox didn't hesitate. He ran down the small stage, his hand still gripping Sienna's. The two rushed past the judges and wedding party, ignoring the protests that came from Jason and Bruce.

Fox pulled Sienna down the hall, loving the way her laughter filled his ears as they headed in the direction of the safe room. Once inside, Fox slammed the door behind them and looked back at Sienna. Her smile was wide and her face bright.

She was beautiful.

"You're full of all kinds of surprises tonight," she said as she caught her breath from their escape.

"I just couldn't do it in there, in front of all the cameras."

Her smile fell. "Do what?"

He reached out and grabbed her hands again. "I know we don't always see eye to eye, and we've made mistakes. But in the short time I've known you, Sienna, you've shown me so much beauty."

She cocked a brow.

"And no, I'm not just talking about your outward beauty, which is great by the way." His face flushed with heat. Getting tongue-tied was not an option right now. "But the way you work so hard toward your goals, and the way you love your sisters, and the way you've opened up to me these past few days. Just being with you makes me feel alive for the first time in what feels like forever. I know we're supposed to go our separate ways in a few days, and I don't know what our future will look like, but I want to find out."

A corner of Sienna's mouth lifted into a small smile.

"I never thought I'd want to date a grumpy old man, and yet, all I want to say is yes."

Fox laughed. "Yeah?"

Sienna nodded.

"So, does that mean I can—"

Sienna cut him off by pressing her lips to his. She wrapped her hands around the back of his neck as he pulled her closer. She smelled like the fresh, green mountain air he loved so much as she molded perfectly into his embrace.

Fox knew they'd have to pay for leaving the set yet again, and he hoped that Eli would understand. But for now, he was happy to have Sienna in his arms and was looking forward to what the future held for them.

## TWENTY-THREE

5 Days Until Dream Wedding

---

SIENNA PRACTICALLY SKIPPED down the stairs to the dining hall the next morning.

After Fox's declaration the night before, she wasn't sure she'd ever leave the safe room. But after way too much kissing, and Harper's persistent banging on the door, the two decided they couldn't hide inside the small room for the next five days.

So, Fox and Sienna had eventually left the linen closet and apologized for running off in the middle of the competition—again. Bruce asked them to return to the meeting room and said all would be forgiven *if* they agreed to do a short on camera interview about what was going on between the two of them.

Apparently, they had enough footage of the two of them together that they wanted to play up this love story in the background of Eli and Audrey's wedding. All in all, it was better than what either of them could hope for.

Sienna checked her reflection in a mirror outside the dining hall to make sure her hair and makeup were the same as they were two minutes ago. Breakfast would technically be her first date with Fox, and she wasn't about to look a mess or show up late.

When she walked through the doorway her gaze immediately found Fox sitting alone at a table in the corner. Not that it was hard. The room was relatively empty. Her sisters hadn't made it down yet, and besides Fox, Harry and Reagan were the only ones in the room. And they were having a tense conversation that Sienna wouldn't interrupt if her life depended on it.

Sienna enjoyed the way Fox watched her as she made her way to the table. She gave him a quick good morning kiss before she sat down. There were two cups of coffee on the table, and a pile of cream and sugar next to Sienna's cup.

He shrugged. "I wasn't sure how you liked it."

Sienna opened one of the small containers of cream and poured it into her drink. "I'm not picky. Just as long as it has caffeine."

"Good to know." Fox chuckled. "I wonder what else I don't know about you."

Sienna squirmed in her seat. As excited as she was to be with Fox, they didn't have all the time in the world to get to know one another. They had five days. "Uh, yeah. But you know this has an expiration date, right?"

Fox smiled. "I know. I spent a lot of time thinking about this last night."

She lifted a brow. "Oh yeah?"

He nodded. "I really like you Sienna. And I don't think five days is enough."

"But I'm going back to the city in five days, and you have your life in Kitty Hawk."

"I don't love it there." He lifted the coffee cup to his lips and took a sip.

"So what? You're going to come to New York with me?" She laughed, but Fox didn't join in.

He held her gaze. "That's exactly what I'm suggesting. I know we don't know each other that well yet, and I'm not saying I think we should move in together. But I don't want to be an eight-hour drive away from you."

Her heart dropped into her stomach. "Are you serious?" The smile that broke out on her face was so big it hurt. "I don't want you to be somewhere you hate."

He shook his head. "Even if I didn't already love New York—which I do—I could never hate anywhere you are."

Well if that wasn't the sweetest thing anyone had ever said to her.

"Are you pulling these lines from movies? These are solid gold. You should consider being a writer."

"Nah, I think I'll stick to singing."

"You want to sing?" Sienna's eyes were wide.

"Well, after the show airs, I'm pretty sure I'll have agents banging down my door," said Fox with a smug shrug. "I'll see if one of them can book you a commercial."

He winked, and she laughed.

New York with Fox was going to be *fun*.

"But seriously, it's because of you that I realized how much I miss it," he said, his eyes going dark and serious —and seriously smoldering. "It's not too late for me to give it another shot. I don't have to have a miserable life just because that's what I've had for the past ten years."

"I made you see that?" Sienna tried unsuccessfully to keep her voice steady.

As she leaned in for another kiss, she wondered how things had changed so quickly. She'd gone from no apartment with a strained relationship with her mother and sisters, to falling for an incredible guy and an exciting new life ahead of her.

Maybe reality shows weren't so bad after all.

Just as Fox's lips found hers, the door to the room banged open.

Harper stood in the doorway, out of breath. "Have either of you seen Audrey this morning?"

Sienna gave her sister the stink eye. "I've been kind of occupied. Isn't she in her room?"

Harper shook her head. "I've looked everywhere. And her car is missing."

Sienna stood up, all thoughts of Fox and New York put on hold.

Tears started to pool in Harper's eyes. And Harper never cried. "I think...I think she's gone."

# Acknowledgments

Daphne and Kayla would like to thank their husbands for putting up with their crazy, and their kids for being so darn adorable.

Thank you Designed with Grace for this amazing cover.

Thank you EditElle for proofreading this book.

And to our AMAZING readers, thank you for letting us keep this dream alive.

# About the Authors

Daphne and Kayla have been writing buddies since 2017.

They have three joint series together, but this is their first cowriting project.

Between the two of them they have: four kids, three cats, two husbands, and one fierce love of writing.

Kayla wishes she could eat tacos every day, and Daphne will never turn down free cake.

You can find them online at:

www.daphnejameshuff.com

www.tirrellblewrites.com

www.ingramcontent.com/pod-product-compliance
Lightning Source LLC
Chambersburg PA
CBHW021153110726
47900CB00002B/546